LADY SARAH'S CHARADE

NANCY RICHARDS-AKERS

AVON BOOKS ◆ NEW YORK

LADY SARAH'S CHARADE is an original publication of Avon Books. This work has never before appeared in book form. This work is a novel. Any similarity to actual persons or events is purely coincidental.

AVON BOOKS
A division of
The Hearst Corporation
1350 Avenue of the Americas
New York, New York 10019

First Avon Books Printing: March 1992

To my (three times) great-aunt Lady Wilkins,
lady-in-waiting to Queen Victoria,
and a grace and favour resident at Hampton Court:

How I wish I might turn back the clock. That not being possible, I visited you in my research. This may be a poor substitute, but I trust it shall pass your heavenly scrutiny.

Earthly Thanks

To the students at Georgetown University whose patience with my children made writing this book possible, especially Molly Manning, Amanda Potts, and Marie Ann Zochowski to whom I wish success in all their future endeavors.

1

A S WAS HER habit, Lady Sarah Clement-Brooke was late. Two platters of frosted almond cakes had been consumed by the guests, rack punch served to the ladies, brandy to the gentlemen, and fifteen pairs of eyes and ears were focused upon the Italian opera singer Amalia Rosetti, who was launching into a piercing soprano aria from *Il Matrimonio Segreto*, as Lady Sarah attempted to slip unnoticed into her aunt's drawing room.

Had it not been for the giant tortoise shell hidden behind the gilt beechwood sofa that entrance might have been an inconspicuous one, but her Aunt Ophelia was forever rearranging her treasures which accounted for the unfortunate presence of the oversized marine relic. Ordinarily, a rather benign collection of miniature Grecian statuary occupied that particular spot. Less frequently, a mahogany box containing a yellowed and much frayed dressing gown reputed to have belonged to Queen Jane Seymour was stored behind the sofa. Thus it was that Lady Sarah, fully expecting to encounter nothing more hazardous than a marble wolfhound, stubbed her satin-slippered toe upon the ill-placed tortoise shell.

"Zeus and Minerva!" the oath escaped before she might check it, and all fifteen pairs of eyes turned to stare at the diminutive young lady as she hopped from one dainty foot to another in a most imprudent fashion.

Lady Ophelia frowned. Had the past twelve years as guardian to her niece been for naught? Granted, she'd owned not a shred of experience regarding the nursery when her older brother and sister-in-law had succumbed to typhus in the Punjab, but she had endeavored to do her best by the girl.

No fussy governess or boarding school for her niece. From the moment the grieving child had stepped off the ship and into her arms, Lady Ophelia had kept Sarah by her side more as a friend and companion than a ward. They lived at her grace and favor residence in Hampton Court, and over the years, Lady Ophelia had shared her interests and hobbies with Sarah; she had taught her mathematics, the Classics, geography and history, both British and Ancient, and she had related every tale in her repertoire about the royal palace in which they were privileged to reside.

While such an upbringing would be considered irregular for the daughter of a peer, it was not, however, noteworthy for the daughter of the Earl of Chelsea. Lady Ophelia, herself the daughter of the sixth earl, had been schooled in all subjects classical and literary, and she was certain her brother would have wished the same for Sarah. Indeed, Lady Ophelia fancied her brother would be much pleased with her efforts as a tutor. Sarah had proven herself more than a mere student; she was a scholar, notably of matters historical.

As for Sarah's aptitude in lessons regarding the social graces, that was another matter altogether. She could neither sing nor play the pianoforte. She loathed the opera and had only a passing interest in the theater. And she was as great a disaster with a needle as she was with watercolors. The list of Sarah's shortcomings was endless. Tardiness; voicing her often radical opinions; more than a touch of indifference regarding feminine concerns such as one's hair style or the fluidity of one's walk; and a total lack of skill in selecting, no less caring about the latest fashion plates. Lady Ophelia's frown deepened.

There were, it appeared, some things that would never change. Hadn't she impressed upon Sarah how important her annual musicale was to her? But look at the girl. Late, again. Her chignon was a sorry sight, having come unpinned so that several wavy locks trailed over each shoulder. And her clothes. She was wearing the same simple round gown of primrose cambric she'd worn this afternoon. Why, there were cobwebs in her hair! Would that the merest iota of those countless speeches on etiquette had made some positive dent in Lady Sarah's unconventional demeanor. Oh, why couldn't the girl have been prompt this one time? Lady Ophelia wondered, unaware that she emitted a tiny moan of distress.

In a nearby upholstered chair, the Honorable Maximillian Carysfort leaned forward to give the lady a comforting pat upon the forearm. "Rosetti's brilliant, my dear. Your guests are, indeed, impressed," he whispered.

While he spoke, he gazed across the room and offered Lady Sarah the variety of indulgent smiles an uncle bestows upon a beloved niece. Although not actually related by blood or marriage, Mr. Carysfort, owing to his long standing friendship with the family, was often called upon to assume the role of older male relative, and it was at times like this that he least relished that role. Reluctantly, his smile vanished, and he gave a curt nod indicating that Lady Sarah locate a seat as quietly and as quickly as possible.

The soprano reached for and held an excruciatingly high-pitched C note, once more commanding the attention of the majority of her audience. A few of the guests, a Mrs. Burges Watson, in particular, did not, however, look away from Lady Sarah, nor did Mrs. Burges Watson bother to disguise her satisfaction that the young woman was once again discrediting herself. Thank goodness the chit was as eccentric a creature as her aunt. If a beauty like Lady Sarah were on the marriage mart, the incurably plain Burges Watson twins would not even stand a chance with the dustman, hence it was a vast relief to their mother that although another Season was commencing Lady Sarah appeared as devoted a bluestocking as always. Indeed, at two-and-twenty, Lady Sarah could definitely be declared on the shelf and quite out of the running.

At the other end of the drawing room, Colonel

Cotton, an officer in the Tenth Dragoons, gave his chum Lord Howland a good-natured jab in the ribs. "Prime article, eh, Howland?" His eyes raked over Lady Sarah, taking in the masses of soft flaxen hair that had escaped the chignon, the wide violet eyes fringed with thick lashes, the cherry ripe mouth, and the tiny, yet shapely female form.

The older gentleman chuckled. "Couldn't agree with you more, and what a pity she's turned out to be as demned queer as her aunt." Howland's gaze shifted to Lady Ophelia. Even at thirty-eight the provocative lines of the older woman's figure enticed a man's imagination. There wasn't a gray hair upon her head, and her wit had become even more delightful with the passage of time. Verily, he had once fancied himself in love with the lady, but she would have none of any gentleman save Carysfort, and even then she had naysayed marriage. There was no understanding the Clement-Brooke women. They'd always been a peculiar lot, over-educated and filled with the most outlandish notions about individuality. Well, Lord Howland deduced, there was likely thin blood in the Clement-Brooke family, and it was just as well the ladies Ophelia and Sarah had never married. What a shame though, two such beauties taking nothing but dusty books to their bedchambers at night.

The soprano finished the aria, and as the guests answered with polite applause the Countess of Mornington raised an ivory-handled lorgnette and turned to her son, the Reverend Gerald Wellesley, resident chaplain of the Chapel Royal at Hampton Court.

"Gel still traipsing after ghosts, is she?" Lady

Mornington's query rose above the dying applause.

"Haven't the foggiest notion, Mother," was the chaplain's lofty reply. He did not intend to be rude, but ghost hunting was a hideously medieval pastime, and Wellesley, who had recently acquired an aversion to gossip, wished to distance himself from the unfortunate topic his mother had chosen to pursue.

The countess was unruffled, and although she realized her son wished her to drop the subject, she had no intention of doing so. "I'll ask the gel myself." Which she did.

Again fifteen pairs of eyes focused upon Lady Sarah.

Not the sort of young lady to know a moment's discomposure, Lady Sarah offered Lady Mornington a quick curtsy and an ebullient reply. "Thank you for asking, ma'am. Yes, I am as you say still traipsing after ghosts. Indeed, I've spent the better part of the day preparing for a vigil in the court below the Silver-Stick Gallery."

"And who is the subject this time, my dear?" The Countess of Mornington who had always owned a fondness for Lady Ophelia was pleased to see that a lady's distinctive qualities had been imparted to her ward. The countess admired a woman who was self-sufficient and did not depend upon a gentleman to enrich her life. The Clement-Brooke ladies were the most fascinating residents of Hampton Court, not a boring bone in either of them, and the countess never tired of their company.

" 'Tis Queen Jane Seymour, ma'am." Sarah blew a stray lock of hair from her eyes and cast a distracted glance about her. "In fact, I was certain

I'd left the dressing gown behind this sofa, but it appears to have moved."

"Not of its own volition, I pray," was Mr. Carysfort's dry injection.

"No, sir." Sarah's violet eyes sparkled at his jest then darted about the drawing room in search of the mahogany box. Lady Ophelia and Sarah occupied a suite of rooms on the first floor of the oldest wing of Hampton Court that had been designed and built for Cardinal Wolsey. At one time, the apartment located off the Base Court had been reserved for visiting heads of state, but when Hampton Court had ceased to be a royal residence and the Lord Chamberlain had begun to assign lodgings to favored persons of rank, Lady Ophelia's great-grandfather had been among the earliest residents. This particularly choice suite of rooms had been occupied by members of the Clement-Brooke family for more than fifty years.

Tonight, Lady Ophelia's guests were gathered in the drawing room which commanded an enviable view of the Old Tudor Gardens and the Thames beyond from its mullioned bay windows. The spacious room was one of the few in the palace which retained its earliest architectural features with linenfold patterned oak walls, a herring-bone brick hearth and elaborate ceiling friezes which displayed Wolsey's badge of cross-keys. History asserted it had once been used by the Constable of France, Duc Anne de Montmorency, upon the occasion of the signing of the marriage treaty for the Princess Mary and Francois I. Now it housed a remarkable array of oddities that chronicled the past three generations of Clement-Brooke family adventures. Most notable was the carved ivory bull which Sarah's great-grandfather had discovered in Ninevah and which was displayed alongside the jewel encrusted double-edged dagger her parents had purchased in the bazaar in Amritsar; on the shelf above the bull and dagger was a graduated line of shiny black and ocher tiger cowry shells which Sarah had gathered on the beach in Madagascar when she was six years old.

But nothing surpassed Lady Ophelia's collection of metaphysical artifacts. For nearly fifteen years, the lady had been engaged in the study and pursuit of the spirits that roamed the galleries, apartments and grounds of Hampton Court, and pursuant to those endeavors she had amassed an extensive array of objects that in some way related to the previous residents of the palace. In addition to Queen Jane's dressing gown, there was a letter written by Anne Boleyn from the Tower, and a lock of Prince Edward's baby hair, which being the most valuable artifacts were kept under lock and key. The other items were displayed for all to admire. There were two soldier's helmets of Cromwell's time that had been discovered alongside skeletons beneath the stones of the Fountain Court; charcoal pencils and an architect's divider had been found in the rooms that had once been Sir Christopher Wren's office; and twenty-eight tinted perfume vials each with a dramatic story about its original owner, her life and demise at the mauve brick palace on the Thames.

"Ah, there it is." Lady Sarah spotted the mahogany box upon a semi-circular table and walked out from the behind the sofa to retrieve it.

"But, my dear, you must explain the whole of it," persisted Lady Mornington. "Why do you need the dressing gown? What is your purpose?"

"Yes, do tell," urged several other guests.

There were few things Sarah enjoyed as much as discussing the history and apparitions of Hampton Court, and she happily commenced an explanation. "As you know Queen Jane's spirit has often been sighted ascending the stairs to the Silver-Stick Gallery."

"Saw her myself," put in Colonel Cotton, who, like most residents of the palace, had encountered at least one of its numerous specters. "She emerged from a doorway to the Queen's apartment with a lighted taper in her hand and proceeded to the staircase. Didn't make a sound and didn't see me either. Looked rather preoccupied. Sad, in fact."

"Precisely, Colonel, and given that sadness and the circumstances of her demise she is a perfect candidate to test our latest theory." Sarah paused, and seeing that she had the rapt attention of everyone in the room, she continued in a much animated voice, "You see, Aunt Ophelia and I have decided the hauntings here at Hampton Court are those of lonely and unhappy spirits. The apparitions are not malicious poltergeists bent on doing evil, rather they're confused souls lost somewhere between life and death. Think, if you will, about poor Queen Jane who had so much to rejoice and live for. The lady had just delivered the heir her king and husband had so desired. She should not have died, and the powers of a terrible grief have shackled her to that spot on earth. It's our further hypothesis that if some of her possessions were to be returned to her she might reconcile her feelings and finally be able to rest in peace."

"And you intend to sit vigil in the gallery this night?"

"Of course."

The Reverend Wellesley remarked beneath his breath about the vulgarity of belief in spirits, and several other ladies fanned themselves frantically, but the Countess of Mornington was neither offended nor unsettled, and she gave Sarah an approving sort of nod.

"Will you visit me in my garden on the morrow? I shall look forward to hearing what transpires during the vigil." The countess, who had lived in the palace since the grace and favor residency of Prince William of Orange, occupied exceedingly choice rooms beneath the Prince of Wales' suite that included a walled garden where she loved to sit and visit with her neighbors.

"I would enjoy it very much, ma'am," was Sarah's sincere answer. Although there were several other young ladies who resided in the palace, Sarah seldom spent any appreciable time in their company. Their minds were filled with naught but talk of marriage and clothes, and as Sarah was little concerned with either, the Countess of Mornington, a venerable lady, who had lived a most fascinating life, here and in Ireland, was a much more stimulating conversationalist.

"Good," Lady Mornington affirmed. "Now that that's in order you must come and sit beside me and tell me what you hear from that brother of yours in Palestine." She indicated an unoccupied chair covered in flowered silk.

Sarah was pleased to oblige, and while she chatted with the countess, the other guests conversed among themselves. Shortly, another round of refreshments was circulated, and Senora Rosetti sang a final aria. Promptly at eleven, the guests departed for their respective apartments scattered throughout the palace and Senora Rosetti was dispatched to accommodations at the nearby Toye Inn before the palace gates were locked for the night. Mr. Carysfort lingered in the drawing room, and Sarah, her smile a bit more knowing than a young lady's ought to be, excused herself so that Lady Ophelia might bid the gentleman a more private good evening.

"Again, you've shown yourself to be one of the palace's finest hostesses. It was a perfect evening, my sweet," Mr. Carysfort said, and Lady Ophelia pulled a skeptical face. "Come now, don't tell me you hold out the slightest expectation that Sarah shall ever change."

"At times such as this, I do."

"She's your mirror image," he said as if no other explanation were necessary.

"But, Max, don't *you* hold out the hope that *I* may change one day?"

"Well aimed, my sweet. You got me on that one." He gave her an affectionate grin. "Tell me, is there still hope I might one day call you wife? And don't ladle me that nonsense about a woman's integrity. You know me well enough that I'd not force you to mend your ways."

"You know, Max, it's been three years since you last talked of marriage," Lady Ophelia remarked, managing to avoid a direct response to his question. "I'd almost given up hope that you'd ever ask me again."

"Have you been waiting?"

"Yes." Of a sudden, there was an uncharacteristic shyness in her demeanor.

He grinned anew. "Ah, my sweet, your words are like succor to a dying man, although why you didn't bring up the subject yourself I can't fathom. Much more your style, I'd warrant."

"Oh, Max, do be serious!"

"Serious, you say! Don't tell me you've finally decided to accept my offer."

Lady Ophelia gave a timid nod to which Mr. Carysfort responded with a whoop of jubilation as he swept her off her feet. "If ever there was a God in Heaven he has seen fit to reward me. When shall it be, my sweet? May? June? As early as possible, I pray."

"Before we set a date it's only fair to tell you there's one condition."

Raising a dark brow, he set her on the floor before him. "Dare I ask?"

"Don't look so suspicious. It's only a little one."

"You'll forgive me, if I reserve judgment," he quipped. "Go on."

"I won't marry until Sarah is wed."

"Egad, a little one, you say! My sweet, you consign me to another twenty years of waiting, if we expect to let Sarah make up her mind in a fashion similar to yours."

"Not if we put our minds to it," she said in a fortifying tone of voice.

"What do you suggest?"

"I'm not certain, but we shall start by submerging ourselves in this Season as we've never done before, and mayhap you can make a trip or two to your club. There must be someone Sarah would not consider conceited, domineering, humorless or frivolous."

"Indeed, there is, but you've already found him."

"Oh, Max, don't tease. I've made up my mind and am quite determined."

"So am I, and as I harbor no greater dream than making you my wife I shall do everything within my power to guarantee your niece is betrothed before this Season's end." Whereupon the gentleman sealed his vow with a kiss.

LADY SARAH'S CHARADE

2

SARA'S FOOTSTEPS, QUICK and purposeful, echoed into the ebony sky as she passed beneath Anne Boleyn's gate and into the Clock Court, so named during the tenancy of Harry the Eighth for the clock His Majesty had installed above the gateway in 1540. The timepiece was an astronomical wonder, telling the number of days since the beginning of the year, the phases of the moon, and the hours at which the moon appears to be highest in the sky, and, hence, the time of high water at London Bridge. All who visited Hampton Court stopped to admire this technical masterpiece, but this evening, Sarah did not glance upward, for her gaze was steadfastly focused upon the opposite side of the quadrangle from which Queen Jane's spirit might soon appear dressed in her white burial shroud.

The April night was seasonably cool, and Sarah

wore a merino cloak with the hood secured over her head; the mahogany box containing Queen Jane's dressing gown was secured beneath her left arm, and in her right hand, she carried a lantern. Earlier in the evening, Sarah had liberally dusted the stairs and passageway to the Queen's apartments with flour, and at the top of the staircase she had rigged a series of fishing nets. The purpose for the flour was to determine whether or not an apparition might leave prints in its wake; the netting was to foil the attempts of pranksters who might try to perpetrate a hoax as the gardener's sons had done several years before. All was in preparation for her vigil, and Sarah had only to lower the lantern flame and position herself in a nearby alcove to wait as she had done on fourteen earlier occasions.

She was halfway to her destination when a movement beneath the arched doorway that led to the Queen's chambers caught her notice. Sarah slipped into the shadows and froze as she watched a figure start up the stairs, then pause. Was it Queen Jane forlornly wandering, as the legend asserted, up and down the stairs seeking something? The figure moved again, this time proceeding up the stairs.

"Oh, no! Come back," Sarah whispered her disappointment aloud as the phantom vanished from her sight. Having no plan, but determined not to loose this chance to have a close encounter with the palace's past, Sarah raced across the quadrangle, darted beneath the arch and lifted her skirts to ascend the stairs in pursuit when the most horrendous noise caused her to drop the mahogany box in fright. A mighty roar, deep pitched and throaty, bellowed through the Clock Court with such ferocity that Sarah determined the being from which it emanated must be of immense size and strength. Wishing to observe this metaphysical being without herself being seen, Sarah ducked behind the nearest portico.

"Christ's nails," came a low male exclamation which was followed by a string of exceedingly indelicate curses.

With the realization that the source of the ruckus was something human, Sarah peered out and gasped as Hessian boots and buff trousers tumbled past her to land in a most undignified heap at the foot of the staircase.

"Well, don't just gape like a tamed monkey! Loose me from this thing," the deep voice ordered.

Sarah, however, did not budge. It was shocking enough to have netted a live gentleman, quite insulting to be compared to a monkey, but nothing matched Sarah's surprise at being ordered about in such a high-handed fashion, and all she could do was continue to stare at the inelegant jumble which was growing angrier by the second.

"I've been waylaid in isolated country inns by calculating mamas, had young ladies fling themselves into my arms only to cry foul, and I've even had more than one scheming ingenue feign impending motherhood, but this is truly the most original attempt to secure an advantageous match to which I've been subjected." His velvety drawl dripped with contempt. "I must congratulate you, my dear girl. At least, you're original."

What in the name of Zeus and Minerva was the man babbling about? Surely, he didn't imagine she had orchestrated this accident? Perhaps the fall had addled his brain. Sarah took a tentative step from behind the portico and held the lantern above her head to enlarge its circle of light.

Before her was a startlingly masculine and undeniably handsome man. Neither his considerable fury nor his marked arrogance, a characteristic Sarah had always considered inexcusable, detracted from the effect of his straight aristocratic nose, strong chin and jaw, brows as dark as midnight, and a full firm mouth. To be sure his was an arresting countenance; in fact, he bore an uncanny resemblance to the marble bust of Hermes in Aunt Ophelia's sitting room, so much so that despite her better judgment Sarah stared at him.

At length, she spoke. "Who are you?"

Disbelief crossed his features. "It's bad enough that you've trussed me up like a pheasant ready for the roasting spit. Please don't play me the fool as well. *You know me*, young lady, as well as *I know your purpose* this night."

"But, sir, I assure you. I've never set eyes on you before."

He gave a derisive snort. "Ah, and how many times have I heard that?"

"I haven't the vaguest notion, and truth to tell, I don't care," she said with such sincerity that the gentleman was taken aback. That toplofty expression seemed to evaporate before her eyes, his midnight black brows pinched together, and he squinted up at her with a look of total incredulity. Sarah could not prevent herself from giggling. It was a quiet giggle, quickly suppressed, but he heard it nonetheless.

His haughty demeanor returned, and he reprimanded, "Hasn't anyone told you it's highly ill-bred to giggle like a serving wench?"

"Not that I can recall," she answered, fighting back the urge to giggle once more, for the scene he presented was quite at odds with his conspicuous sense of self-importance. His long legs were entwined in the fishing nets, his neckcloth was askew, his hair mussed, and what was likely one of Weston's finest frock coats was smudged with flour as was the tip of his nose. Having triumphed over the giggles, she went on, "I ought to be quite furious at you, sir, for daring to call *me* ill-bred, but I find this situation far too ridiculous to take serious offense at *your* ill-bred remarks. Really, sir, have you any idea what a comical sight you present?"

For the first time the gentleman glanced down at himself, and after several fruitless attempts to remove the netting from about his legs, a small smile teased the edges of his full mouth. "Most undignified, I fear."

She couldn't resist offering a smile of her own. "I shan't tell a soul, if you don't."

"We've a bargain. But I do have one question. If not myself, who were you attempting to trap? For this is certainly what I've fallen into."

"The gardener's sons."

"Ah, so you did have matrimony in mind."

"Really, sir," Sarah's voice was heavy with disdain, "You lack manners to speak as if I were some dairy maid casting eyes at the farmer's son. The fact is I was engaged in a serious scientific endeavor which I fear you've quite ruined."

"Scientific endeavor?"

"Indeed. This, sir, is the staircase to the Silver-Stick Gallery, the haunt of Queen Jane Seymour."

"Don't tell me you're ghost hunting!"

"Don't sound so flabbergasted." She raised her delicate nose several degrees skyward. "It's a far more worthwhile pursuit than curricle racing on the Dover Road or wagering outrageous sums on trivia such as whether or not a particular lady's hair color is natural."

"Do I detect a note of condescension?"

The conversation wasn't going anywhere. It was like talking to one of the Burges Watson twins, and finding she had had quite enough bantering, Sarah turned away.

"Don't go yet. You must help me out of this." Only as an after-thought did he add, "Please."

As it was the civil thing to do, Sarah agreed. Bending down, she first unraveled the net, then she extended a helping hand to the gentleman, and in the next instant, he towered over Sarah requiring her to arch her neck in order to look him in the face. The hood of her cloak fell back to reveal her delicate face, tiny upturned nose and an abundance of flaxen hair, loosely gathered at the nape of her neck and tumbling about her shoulders.

Transfixed by this provocative sight, the gentleman studied her, imagining how soft that hair must be, wondering if she bathed in scented waters and if those tresses might smell of roses or violets. He had always had a special fondness for the sweet jasmine fragrance of vernal roses, and the thought of running his hands though that hair and inhaling the heady aroma of roses made his blood race dangerously. In a husky voice, he asked, "You're certain we've never met?"

Unaware of the direction of his thoughts, Sarah smiled. "Quite positive."

"Perhaps we should rectify that unfortunate error," he drawled in that velvety smooth voice and gave her a lazy grin the effect of which made Sarah's heart lurch.

She held her breath. He stepped closer. And while she wondered what might happen next he reached out a hand and swept the hair from her temples, next he cradled her face in both hands, leaned down and kissed her soundly on the lips. What started as a gentle touch began to deepen, and Sarah trembled like an aspen leaf, her eyelashes fluttered closed, and a small inarticulate sound escaped her.

Nothing like this had ever happened to her before, and she was overwhelmed by wave upon wave of unfamiliar sensations. First, she was hot, then cold, and then she was hot again. The heat from his body warmed her, and she discovered herself pressing closer to his firm chest, as if she might melt into him. Her body was tingling, her head was spinning, and suddenly, she was seized by the awful sensation of falling in a dream. She regained control of herself with a jolt.

"Loose me this instant, you pompous peacock!"

The novelty of being called a pompous peacock caused the gentleman to throw back his head and surrender to hearty laughter. "Madame, I concede." Giving a roguish grin, he executed a gallant bow. "Though you must admit 'twas a most pleasant interlude."

"Pleasant?" was her immediate retort. Indignation sharpened her voice. "Sir, you're far too bold to presume what I might consider pleasant. Indeed, I fear vanity has impeded your ability to think clearly."

The gentleman was not fazed by this, and to Sarah's outrage that roguish grin deepened as he turned on his heels and bounded up the stairs. At the top he paused and called down in a teasing voice, "Farewell, mysterious lady of the night, if we never meet again in this life, I'm sure you shall track me down in the after world." Then he vanished into the darkness of the Silver-Stick Gallery.

Sarah stamped her foot in aggravation. *Pompous peacock* was hardly the half of it! He was audacious and he was . . . *He*, but who was he? She listened to the fading echo of his footsteps. And where was he going? The footsteps died away, and she raised her hand to brush her fingertips across her slightly swollen lips. Would she ever see him again?

Zeus and Minerva, why was she even giving the rogue a second thought? An inner voice snapped her back to reality. The gentleman possessed the most gargantuan ego of any individual she had ever encountered. He was rude and brazen and more than a bit domineering, and he certainly was not the sort of individual whose company Sarah normally desired. But that kiss made all his faults seem sadly insignificant. Sweet Lord, that kiss. Would she ever forget how it had made her feel?

Granted, she'd never been kissed before, but that inexperience should not account for the dizzying affect his touch had produced. Should it? Those brief seconds in his arms had been luscious and heady and more than a little frightening. It was troubling to admit there was something or, in this case, someone, which had caused her logical brain to lapse into momentary discomposure.

Sarah sighed, and shook her head in an attempt to purge all distracting thoughts, but it was to no avail. Nothing but an image of Hermes's face swam before her mind's eye. It appeared, for this night at least, Sarah had lost all interest in Queen Jane, and she picked up the mahogany box to return to Lady Ophelia's apartment.

3

ALL SIX FEET, two inches of Beverly Edward Christian Carysfort, the Right Honorable Earl of Radnor, were sprawled across a gold and maroon striped sofa. One leg was flung over a carved arm rest, his stockinged foot dangling in the air, while the other leg was propped upon a chair his lordship had pushed beside the sofa.

The gentleman gave a tortured moan. Who in the blazes had pulled back the curtains? It couldn't be noon yet, and having no intention of opening his eyes until a more civilized hour, the earl plopped onto his side and buried his head beneath the nearest needlepoint pillow. He had come to Hampton Court for peace and quiet, but his final thought as he drifted back to sleep was that thus far his retreat from Society had been less than satisfying.

A few paces from the gold and maroon sofa,

Maximillian Carysfort relaxed in an armchair and read a copy of yesterday's *Gazette*. Although it was not the usual course of events to awaken and discover the Earl of Radnor collapsed upon the sofa in one's sitting room, it was Mr. Carysfort's daily habit to relax before the open window, read his paper and enjoy a strong cup of Java coffee, and nothing would deter him from that routine. Having enjoyed a good chuckle over the latest political cartoons, he set the *Gazette* aside and studied his nephew with a calculating eye.

Radnor was a tall gentleman with square shoulders, narrow hips and lean muscular legs; this natural athletic appearance having been greatly enhanced by hours spent perfecting his boxing stance at Gentleman Jim's. The earl was a renowned Corinthian, a relentless sportsman of unsurpassed talents, who despite his compelling good looks, ancient title, vast estates and sizable fortune, remained unwed. This was, perhaps, of all his accomplishments the most notable, given that he had been considered the most desirable marriage catch for more than nine seasons, yet had neither succumbed to Cupid's dart nor the machinations of more than one over-zealous parent. Radnor was going to be thirty-two this summer, an age when most gentlemen already had at least one or two offspring populating the nursery, but he was no closer to having an heir than the day he'd departed Cambridge.

Mr. Carysfort turned back to the *Gazette*. None of the news was uplifting. Bonaparte was again in Paris, readying his army; Robert Owen's latest essay was calling for the abolition of the state lottery; and there were grizzly reports on the death of a chimney sweep and the execution of a pickpocket. Mr. Carysfort glanced back at the earl, and in the hopes of rousing him, he shook the paper several times. The younger man, however, was unperturbed by this feeble attempt to provoke him, whereupon Mr. Carysfort set his coffee cup upon its saucer with an over-loud clatter which managed to produce a slight twitching in the earl's shoulders as his head inched farther beneath the needlepoint pillow.

"Ahem." Mr. Carysfort's curiosity as to why his nephew was asleep on his sofa demanded to be satisfied. Being only ten years his senior, they had grown up more like siblings, and Mr. Carysfort couldn't help wondering what scrap the earl had landed himself in. He recalled their younger days on the Town and fancied that it must have something to do with the weaker sex. "Ahem," he repeated in a considerably louder voice.

The earl groaned. "Quarter, Max." He rolled to his back and as the needlepoint pillow fell to the floor he flung an arm across his face to block out the sunlight.

Mr. Carysfort smiled. "Good morning, Bev. Haven't seen you since Twelfth Night. To what do I owe this unexpected visit? No one's died at Temple Radnor have they?"

"Can't you be serious, Max? I've come for your help, not your humor, and most especially not at this ungodly hour. Can't you close that curtain?"

"Certainly not. The hour's not ungodly, and if you're feeling under the weather, a bit of sunshine will do you a world of good."

"I'm not sick."

"You were doing a fairly competent imitation," Mr. Carysfort shot back, then softened his tone to add, "Sorry, old chap. What's the problem? You know I'll do whatever I can to help you out of a bind. You haven't got some female in a peculiar situation, have you?"

The earl choked. "I *have not*."

"What plagues you then?"

He heaved a sigh of which Edmund Kean himself would have been proud. "Another Season is about to descend upon us and again I already find myself the object of the most appalling ploys. It's one thing when one's popularity means seldom passing a solitary night, but it's quite another matter when it makes day-to-day existence a veritable obstacle course," he lamented. "Every female in Town, it seems, would be my wife, and they would resort to any odious trick to make it possible."

Mr. Carysfort burst into gales of laughter. "What do you expect? And don't, I caution, be so swell-headed as to attribute your woes to your fine figure or manly good looks. The truth is you're eligible and a confirmed bachelor. The combination's irresistible. Egad, don't tell me I forgot to warn you about the unfortunate penchant toward improvement of the male species that lurks beneath every woman's bodice. Not only are you ideal marriage material, you're ripe for reformation." This remark appeared to cause the earl to frown, but as his arm remained across his face, Mr. Carysfort was not certain of the younger gentleman's precise expression. "Must I converse with your arm? It's very rude and most disconcerting, you know."

"Sorry, Max." The earl sat up, swung his long muscular legs over the side of the sofa and stretched.

"Coffee?" The older gentleman indicated the silver tray set upon the nearby table with coffee service and freshly baked muffins in a basket that was fashioned of woven silver and gold strings.

"Yes, thank you." The earl helped himself to a cup and enjoyed several sips before the conversation resumed.

"The purpose of your visit is, I gather, to seek refuge?"

"On the mark." The earl paused in the business of slathering a muffin with black currant preserves to punctuate this statement by jabbing the air with the butter knife. "Oh, I suppose I could have travelled to Sussex and set up housekeeping at Temple Radnor for the next few weeks, but, the truth is, I've met the loveliest Russian ballet dancer and frankly was loath to put too much distance between the two of us. May I stay, Max?"

"Of course, but what's so wrong with marriage? Not to the ballet dancer, of course, but to one of the new Season's offerings?"

"*You* can ask that?"

Mr. Carysfort grinned like a schoolboy. "The lady has finally accepted my suit, so don't point a finger at me."

"Lady Ophelia has agreed to marry you?" The earl could not have been more astounded had he read an announcement of his own betrothal in the *Times*.

"That she did, and just last night." He neglected, of course, to mention the condition Lady Ophelia had attached to their betrothal. There was no sense in putting a blot on his good news.

The earl stood and embraced his uncle. "Congratulations. Have you set a date?"

"Not yet. But come, Bev, don't stray from the subject at hand. We were talking of you and marriage. What I do with my life is no point of comparison for yourself, for I didn't inherit the title. Whether or not a fifth son ever amounts to anything is of little concern. You, however, being the eldest son of an eldest son inherited the title, and what you do is of great concern to all of us."

"Egad, Max, cut line. You're sounding like grandmother. You know, there's no female alive who holds my affections more dearly than your mother, and while I'm most loath to disappoint the dear lady, the fact is I can live my life for no one save myself."

"Yet you'd let her go to the grave without seeing her fondest wish become a reality."

"Grandmother's ill?"

"Nothing more than her usual gout."

"Then stop overstating the case. Don't worry, Max, I shan't let down eighteen generations of Carysforts. The title will remain in the family."

Raising a skeptical brow, Mr. Carysfort's words were dry. "I'm sure the ground beneath the graveyard at Temple Radnor has stilled noticeably."

"You'd hardly expect me to jump into something as momentous as matrimony with just anyone."

"Hardly," he rejoined in an even drier tone.

"Just my point," the earl said eagerly.

"Although you must admit, it's high time for you to stop being quite so picky."

"I suppose you're right." He resumed slathering preserves on the muffin. "I mean I don't have to fall in love with the lady, merely find her somewhat agreeable to the eye and suitable to be my countess and mother for an heir."

Mr. Carysfort was genuinely appalled. "When did you become such a cynic? You needn't be quite so calculating."

The earl shrugged and popped a piece of muffin in his mouth.

"What in heaven's name happened to your coat?" Mr. Carysfort noticed the bottle-green frock coat smudged with flour.

"It was the most extraordinary thing. I quite literally stumbled across a young woman engaged in ghost hunting."

"Ghost hunting? You don't say," Mr. Carysfort remarked as if he had no notion of what the earl could be talking about. His eyes, however, belied far more excitement than his voice, for they twinkled with the birth of an idea. Wouldn't it be perfect if his nephew and Lady Ophelia's niece were to develop a tendre for one another?

"Yes, and she was quite the most outspoken female I've ever encountered. The palace must be overrun with such unusual types. From my last visit, I seem to recall most of the residents either had one foot in the grave or were the most formidable ape leaders."

Mr. Carysfort schooled his tone to sound as nonchalant as possible. "Not really. I believe I know the particular lady of whom you speak, and I assure you she's one of a kind."

"You must be right. It's certainly the first time I've been called a pompous peacock."

"A what? Oh, no, Beverly. What did you do?"

"Nothing unpardonable. Merely impulsive. I stole a kiss. There we were beneath the shelter of an archway in the deserted Clock Court, the moon was high, we were all alone. Why, what would you have done, uncle? And if you know the lady of whom I speak, then you must admit she does have the most astonishingly glorious hair."

Mr. Carysfort chuckled. Oh, this was splendid. Beverly and young Sarah together last night! While his more paternal side trusted it had been nothing more than a quick kiss, he could not help hoping the seed of some deeper attraction had been sown. "Yes, indeed, Bev, you're most welcomed to stay with me. Stay as long as you like."

"I knew I could count on you. Thanks, Max. Now tell me, what do you do around here for amusement?"

"Sorry to say I've got an engagement this morning," replied Mr. Carysfort. He was anxious to visit Lady Ophelia and tell her about his nephew's serendipitous arrival. "But I shall show you around this afternoon. There's a tennis court you might enjoy, and an extensive stud. In the meantime, I suggest you pay a courtesy call upon the Countess of Mornington."

"Wellington's mother?"

He nodded in the affirmative.

"Egad, the lady must be ninety, if she's a day."

"Almost. However, she's sharp as a tack, and as she's rather the reigning patroness of our little Society here it would be only proper that you pay your respects. Besides think how safe you'll be in her company," quipped Mr. Carysfort, fully aware that Sarah had agreed to visit the countess this morning. Oh, how he wished he might be a beetle in the countess's flower garden. The reunion between Sarah and Radnor was bound to be an intriguing one.

4

SARAH SAT CROSS-legged at the end of Lady Ophelia's tent bed, her back was propped against one of the reeded posts about which pristine white muslin hangings were draped. It was a beautiful spring morning. Sunlight streaked across the apricot satin counterpane, the yellow canary in its gilt cage was warbling a cheery tune, and the sweet fragrance from woodbine climbing up the wall outside the open window drifted through the room. The ladies were lingering over cups of frothy Holland chocolate, a practice which they had enjoyed from the first day Sarah had come to live with Lady Ophelia and which was as a rule accompanied by an animated recitation of past or upcoming events by Sarah. This morning, however, Sarah's usual enthusiasm was absent. The young lady was unnaturally distressed.

"There will always be other nights," Lady Ophelia reassured from her lacy nest of pillows. She offered her niece a soothing smile. "You mustn't trouble yourself that nothing was accomplished."

"But you've been so dedicated, Aunt Ophelia, and I hate to let you down like this."

"Nonsense. You should know by now that the unexpected is always to be expected, particularly in this line of exploration. Besides, from all you've told me, the accident wasn't your fault."

Feeling distinctly uneasy, Sarah focused upon the rim of the delft blue porcelain cup two inches away from her nose. She had not told Aunt Ophelia everything that had happened last night. She'd hardly told her the half of it, and Sarah wasn't sure why, for she'd done nothing wrong. Not even the kiss was anything to fret over. It had been bound to happen sooner or later; even she could not expect to pass her entire life without a single kiss from a gentleman. Furthermore, as the gentleman had probably returned to his home where ever that might be, the encounter was already in the past, and she would do best to banish it from her thoughts.

Despite this impeachable logic Sarah could not dismiss the feeling that something had changed, and she feared that to begin to relate the whole of last night to Aunt Ophelia would require mention of certain things she didn't understand. Of course, Sarah was a realist. She knew nothing remained the same, and she accepted the fact that she was bound to change as the years passed, but right now she wasn't ready to think about the future.

Lady Ophelia set her chocolate on the bedside table. She couldn't recall the last time Sarah had been this preoccupied. Had it been three years ago when she had proved the haunting in the King's Audience Chamber was a hoax? Or was it the time she had grappled with the decision whether or not to leave Hampton Court to live with her brother Simon in Palestine? Both events had tested Sarah's character. Surely, she wasn't taking the disrupted vigil *that* seriously. Never one to force an issue Lady Ophelia knew her niece would confide in her sooner or later. In the meantime, she intended to divert Sarah's thoughts and raise her spirits with her good news. "I've something special to tell you that I trust shall brighten your day."

Sarah looked up in expectation. "Yes?"

"Mr. Carysfort and I are to be married."

"Oh, that is superlative news." A genuine smile brightened Sarah's countenance, and she scooted across the counterpane to give her aunt a hug and a kiss to each cheek. "I'm thrilled for you and Mr. Carysfort."

As if she had not heard Sarah's enthusiasm, Lady Ophelia hastened to put in, "You mustn't worry that this means you shall be thrust out into the world on your own. I expect Max and I shall live in his suite, and you, of course, will remain with us, or perhaps, you'd like this apartment. You're old enough, y'know. Of age and in control of your own purse."

Sarah was puzzled by the course of the conversation. "Aunt Ophelia, you mustn't concern yourself with me at a time like this. You're to be a bride which I imagine is the one time in a lady's life when she may surrender to the sinful pleasure of being the center of attention." She gave Lady Ophelia another hug. "Oh, I'm so very happy for you."

"You're not just saying that for my benefit, are you?"

"How could you ask?"

Lady Ophelia hesitated in her reply, and as Sarah regarded her aunt comprehension dawned across the younger lady's delicate countenance.

"Oh, no, dear aunt, please don't tell me one of the reasons you ever delayed marrying was because of me!" Sarah was visibly horrified. "I could not bear to think I kept you from your happiness."

"No, my dear, you did no such thing." The words were scarcely spoken before Lady Ophelia experienced the most dreadful attack of guilt. She was not lying to Sarah. Not precisely. She was merely omitting a few facts and would continue to do so. She was not going to utter a single word about *the condition*. If the girl were already blue-deviled about something, that would certainly send her off into the tree tops. "Although I must confess to an excess of rather maternal concerns about your future, the reasons were mine alone. I wasn't ready. Though what that precisely means I cannot say, for I've loved Max from the start." She puzzled over this for a few seconds, then added, "Please promise me that if you ever fall in love you won't let *anything* stand in the way. There's so little time in this world, and we must not waste a moment of it."

Sarah had seldom heard her aunt talk in such a serious vein. "I promise nothing shall stand in the way, although I fear the prospect of falling in love is a rare one in my case."

A tiny frown knit Lady Ophelia's brow. They had not talked much about love or marriage or the nature of a relationship between a man and a woman, and Lady Ophelia supposed that she had done the girl a grave injustice, but until now it had seemed like everything else was more important. She had taught Sarah independence and self-confidence, and how to be assertive without giving offense; the girl had a lively curiosity, excellent intellect and a sharp wit. It wasn't that Lady Ophelia had disdained Society or matrimony, rather those were things that had held no place in her life. She and Sarah had been busy, their lives had been full and neither had paused to search for anything more. Until now.

Of late, Lady Ophelia had known a peculiar nagging, a sort of funny little lonely spot within her. It had started this past Christmas Eve when she had watched the village children dressed as angels and it had gotten progressively worse with the births of Lady Pakenham's daughter and the Arbuthnot heir. She had to admit something was absent from her life, and an inner sense told her that marrying Max was the right thing to do. At least it was the right thing for herself. But what about Sarah? Although she was younger than herself was it possible that Sarah could come to feel this way?

Hoping that it wasn't too late, Lady Ophelia said, "Of course, you've had little chance to meet any eligible young gentlemen here."

"That's not true. I've met numerous young men whom I'm certain represent a fair sampling of those I'd encounter should I ever seek a voucher to Almack's. Don't say you've already forgotten Sir Walter Scott's nephew, Andrew, who joined us for tea one afternoon and treated us to a recitation of the most pedantic *Ode to a Mauve Palace*. And, of course, there have been the annual autumn holiday visits by Viscount Dufferin's grandsons, and even the Countess of Mornington has trotted out a veritable army of Wellesley relatives. Not a single one of them has been the least bit intriguing." Even as she spoke Sarah mentally corrected herself. They'd all been uninspiring. All but one. While the gentleman last night did not qualify as a social acquaintance, he most assuredly qualified as intriguing. "Should I ever fall in love it will certainly never be with someone as hideously boring as Andrew Scott."

As always Sarah was decisive in her opinion, and Lady Ophelia smiled with affection, but in the next instant that smile faded away, for Lady Ophelia could not help wishing Sarah was just a wee bit enamored with the notion of marriage for its own sake. While she had accepted Mr. Carysfort's proposal, she had been quite serious about the condition, and no matter how strong her love might be, she would not marry before Sarah had, and so she launched her campaign to find a suitable husband for Sarah:

"Wouldn't you like a Season, Sarah?" It was more of an offer than a question.

"What a terrible waste," replied Sarah, who was somewhat bewildered that her aunt would suggest such a thing since she was past the age of coming out.

"Fustian. There's no reason why you shouldn't indulge, if you wish. We've plenty of funds."

"It's kind of you to offer, but I couldn't imagine myself partaking of all that folderol."

"Well, mayhap you'll decide to participate in just a few of the Season's social events. We've received an invitation from Lord and Lady Anglesea for their annual ball. You've never been before, but I'm feeling in a celebratory mood. Would you agree to go with Max and me?"

"If it would make you happy, of course, I'll attend."

"Yes, it would make me happy. Most prodigiously so. And 'tis most unselfishly wonderful of you to agree." Lady Ophelia felt as if she'd taken the first step down the aisle in the Chapel Royal, and she couldn't wait to tell Max that, as a beginning, Sarah had consented to attend the Anglesea ball. "Now I must see to my correspondence. Are you off to visit with Lady Mornington?"

"Yes, although I fear she shall be most disappointed in the turn of events."

"Perhaps not. The countess loves a good story and the events of last night are prime tattle. Who knows, she may even be able to reveal the identity of the gentleman. Aren't you in the least bit curious about him?"

"Yes," replied Sarah, managing to disguise the full extent of her inquisitiveness. It was perturbing to be intrigued by a gentleman, and denying the truth was Sarah's way of downplaying the significance of such a development.

"Personally, I'd be mad to know everything. Tell me, was he handsome?"

"I didn't notice," was her offhand reply. She observed Lady Ophelia, then asked, "Besides, what sort of question is that?"

"A romantic one, of course." Lady Ophelia heaved a dramatic sigh and then dimpled like a mischievous schoolgirl. "It must be my mood."

"Then there's no need to summon the leech," Sarah teased.

"No, I shall recover. Now off with you until teatime. Max will be joining us."

After stopping by her room to put on a bonnet, Sarah chose the outside route through the Privy Gardens of deep evergreen yews to reach the Countess of Mornington's suite at the north-east corner of the palace. She edged the Great Fountain Garden and soon arrived at her destination, where the Tudor north front of Cardinal Wolsey met the classical addition of Sir Christopher Wren.

From where Sarah stood on the pebbled walkway, Lady Mornington's thin, yet commanding voice could be heard rising over the garden wall.

"The ability to see ghosts seems to be a gift granted to very few people," she was explaining to someone.

Sarah wondered who Lady Mornington's visitor might be, and without hesitation she knocked on the high gate, then opened the door and entered. The countess and her guest were seated in "Purr Corner," the warm nook so-named by one of her sons because it was a favorite cose of his mother's septuagenarian female visitors. A tea tray was set upon an ornate table inlaid with mother-of-pearl, a gift her eldest son had acquired while governor of Madras, and the countess was handing a cup to a gentleman seated on her right.

Something inside Sarah's chest gave a lurch. It was the gentleman from last night, and he was more handsome than she had remembered. Hermes with midnight hair and very masculine yet aristocratic features. His blue morning coat was stretched without a wrinkle across his broad shoulders, cream colored pantaloons encased legs that were longer and more muscular than she recalled, but it was those eyes beneath ink-black brows which, revealed for the first time in the light of day, caused something else to flutter in her chest. They were the same clear blue color of the Aegean Sea. Having sailed those waters as a young girl, Sarah knew the hue well and the opaque beauty of his eyes captivated her as the swirling waters had done.

He rose, his gaze met hers, and the roguish grin dancing in those clear blue eyes caused a pink blush to suffuse her cheeks. She didn't even know the gentleman's name, but he made her feel as if he could read her inner-most thoughts. Sweet heaven, he wasn't thinking about that kiss, was he?

"Lady Sarah, my dear child, I've been expecting you. I don't believe you know my visitor, although I understand you've already encountered one another. My dear, may I present the Earl of Radnor. My lord, Lady Sarah Clement-Brooke."

The earl made an elegant bow and spoke in a tone of dawning enlightenment. "Why, you must be Lady Ophelia's niece. I should have known."

"You're acquainted with my aunt?" was Sarah's incredulous rejoinder. Surely Aunt Ophelia didn't count such a conceited coxcomb among her acquaintances.

"Of course, Maximillian Carysfort is my uncle. I've come to visit for a while."

"I see," she said, coming to the realization that this gentleman was probably going to join their daily tea, and it would be starve or suffer his company.

Lady Mornington observed this exchange through her raised lorgnette. Having passed three-quarters of a century on this earth, the lady easily recognized the signs of attraction between a man and a woman, and she knew a warming in her heart that the independent Lady Sarah was as susceptible to a handsome gentleman as any other young lady might be. Although the countess considered self-reliance a virtue, she considered life devoid of romance to be a tragedy. It was long past time for Radnor to settle down and have an heir, the countess mused. Mayhap, the gentleman had finally met his match in the singular Lady Sarah.

"Come, my dear Sarah, do join us. Ah, how fortunate I am to receive visits from two of the more interesting young people I've ever known. And at the same time." As soon as Sarah was seated upon the wrought-iron bench on the other side of the countess, the lady went on, "Lord Radnor has told me about last evening, and while I'm sorry to learn you did not espy Queen Jane, his tale was, I assure you, just as diverting."

Inadvertently, Sarah's hand rose to her lips. Precisely *what* had he told Lady Mornington?

Noticing her apprehension, the earl spoke in a meaningful tone, "Rest assured, Lady Sarah, I took all the blame."

How unusually reasonable, thought Sarah while she assumed a sweet smile and said, "Thank you, sir. You're most gallant."

"Yes, isn't he? See, Sarah, you must not worry, my dear. I doubt Jane Seymour is going anywhere, and there shall always be another night. Besides I've a new and most promising lead for you. Are you familiar with the Old Court House down by the water's edge?"

"It was the home of Sir Christopher Wren, was it not?" the earl, who had excelled in his studies of British architectural history while at Cambridge, queried.

"Indeed, and he died in the dining room," supplied Sarah. "For the past seven years it's been the home of Major Lord Hugh and Lady MacGregor."

"And of late there have been suspicious noises in the house," said the countess. "My dresser has heard from their cook that doors have been slamming shut and footsteps have been heard on the staircase during the night and daylight hours."

"During the daylight hours, you say. That is most fascinating, ma'am. Although spirits are generally known to roam at dusk or after the sun has set, Aunt Ophelia says a daylight haunting is possible, but we've never encountered one ourselves. Do you know how frequently they've occurred?"

"Rather often, I fear. Verily, some of the servants have been quite frightened, and Lady MacGregor is most perturbed since several have threatened to leave her employ."

"That is unfortunate. I'm sure Aunt Ophelia will wish to commence an investigation straight away."

The conversation then turned to Lady Mornington's offspring, in particular her fifth son, Arthur, the Duke of Wellington. Word of Bonaparte's recent escape from Elba had shocked the nation, and barely three weeks had passed since the duke had agreed to command an allied army in Brussels. Two days earlier the countess had received a brief missive from her son, and she shared with her visitors

Wellington's recounting of the problems with the soldiers under his command, most of whom did not speak a word of English, and of the social life in the foreign capital, in particular the Countess of Richmond's grand ball that had been scheduled for mid-June.

Sarah and the earl were fascinated by this intelligence, and in turn they plied the countess with questions. Eventually, the earl glanced at the time piece he carried in his waistcoat pocket. Far more time than the fifteen minutes which etiquette allowed for such a visit had elapsed.

"My lady, this has been a delightful morning, but I've woefully over-stayed my welcome."

Sarah was equally apologetic. "I, too, seem to have lost track of time, ma'am. Please forgive me."

Lady Mornington waved an impatient hand, first to her left, then to her right. "Don't babble on like a pair of ninnies. Sarah, you especially should know there's no need for such formality with me. I do, however, find myself somewhat fatigued otherwise you could stay all day as far as I'm concerned. Silly rule that fifteen minute thing. You'll return soon I trust. Both of you," she stressed.

"Yes, ma'am." Sarah stood and gave the elderly lady a curtsy.

The earl bowed to the countess, then addressed Sarah. "Might I walk you back to your aunt's apartment, Lady Sarah?"

"Now don't be shy, my dear, I'm sure your aunt would approve. Besides he's a most desirable catch."

"So I'm led to believe," was Sarah's wry comment. Noting the faint tinge of what must have been a blush upon the earl's forehead, she felt a stab of remorse. "Thank you, my lord, I should appreciate that."

A servant assisted the elderly lady inside her apartment, and Lady Sarah and the earl departed.

"The countess is quite an astonishing lady," remarked Lord Radnor.

Sarah agreed. "When I reach her age I should like to be half that spry."

"I should like to reach her age," the earl rejoined with a laugh. He let his gaze linger on the radiant young woman beside him and he realized with a jolt that she both intrigued him and stirred his blood. "I was rather overbearing last evening. Please accept my profound apologies, Lady Sarah."

She cast a sideways glance at the earl as if to measure the sincerity of his statement, and, faced with a contrite smile, she grinned back. "I accept your apology, sir, and tender one of my own."

"Excellent. I should be pleased, if we might start anew, for it would trouble our respective relatives, if we were to be at odds over anything as unimportant as last evening. After all it was nothing more than an unfortunate accident, and accidents do happen."

His casual reference to the events of last night as nothing more than an accident caused Sarah to wince inwardly. It should not have been a surprise that the kiss had meant nothing to him. The earl was a gentleman of experience. Likely, he'd kissed scores of young ladies. But instead of being a comfort, Sarah found this thought most depressing, and there was an absurd trembling in her lower lip which required several moments to get under control. At length, she said, "I quite agree on all points, sir."

"Even if I'm a preening peacock?"

In spite of herself she gave a spontaneous laugh. "It may be that I mistook you, my lord. I've the highest respect for the Countess of Mornington's opinion and know that lady owns not the slightest patience for fools."

"So it's on her account we start anew," he reflected.

"In part."

"There's something else?"

"Your sense of humor, my lord."

He raised an inquisitive brow.

"You had the soundness of mind to laugh at yourself last evening," Sarah expanded. "A rare quality and one I find most admirable."

"I shall keep that in mind."

They walked several paces in silence broken only by the hum of an errant bee as they passed beside a fragrant clump of verbena.

"Are you familiar with the palace?" she asked.

"Not really. The last time I visited must have been eight or nine years ago, and I haven't seen much other than Max's apartment, and, of course, the staircase to the Silver-Stick Gallery."

His remark caused a blush to color Sarah's cheeks, and for a moment she almost refrained from voicing her offer.

"I'd be pleased to show you a few of the more notable features."

"I would appreciate that," he accepted without the slightest hesitation. For many years, the earl had wished to tour the palace, but such a sedentary activity was considered unfashionable by his Corinthian set, and the earl, who had a reputation to maintain, did not wish to incur the scorn of his cronies.

Proceeding the long way around to the old gate near the foot of the wooden bridge, Sarah pointed out the Wilderness and its Lion Gates and Maze, which upon being asked she promised to show the earl at another time.

As they strolled Sarah explained some of the history of the palace and its hauntings.

"One night when the gatekeeper was closing up he looked down the Broad Walk and saw six figures, three gentlemen and three ladies, approaching." She paused to determine whether or not he was interested. His absorbed expression encouraged her to continue, "Thinking they were residents returning from an evening social event he waited to lock the gates until they had entered. As they came closer he saw they were in costumes as of Tudor times. They didn't make a sound, but waved their arms as if beckoning to the gatekeeper, who followed them into the old Dutch Garden whereupon they vanished into thin air."

"You're quite serious about this ghost hunting," he remarked.

"Is that disapproval I hear, my lord?"

"No, it's not disapproval. As you say it's more worthwhile than curricle racing. What you heard is astonishment mingled with disbelief, for I can't recall ever having met another young lady with an interest that wasn't dedicated to her personal vanity or to—"

"A devious intent to trap you into marriage,"

Sarah was unable to resist the impulse to inject.

"You don't really believe I've been subject to such tactics, do you?"

"I suppose it must be true, for I've endured a few afternoon teas in the company of the Burges Watson twins and was treated to an earful of such things."

"Pray, don't tell me these young ladies reside in grace and favor at the palace."

"Regretfully, they do, but they're not terribly bright, and I promise to warn you straightaway should I hear of any hatchling plots."

"I believe you're making fun of me."

"Not entirely."

Wishing to know more about this singular young woman, the earl redirected the conversation. "What is your next project, Lady Sarah? Shall you return to the Clock Court?"

"My vigils always coincide with the dates upon which there have been previous sightings, hence I shall not hope to see Queen Jane for another four months. In the meantime, I shall pursue the stories of which Lady Mornington spoke. The first step shall be to confer with Aunt Ophelia, then interview the servants at the Old Court House, after which we shall hopefully arrange a series of vigils to document the noises."

"Would you mind if I accompanied you?"

"On the vigils?"

"The interviews as well. There doesn't appear to be much else to do here, and truth to tell, I find your hobby most diverting."

"I don't know any reason why not," she replied somewhat cautiously. While she found she liked the earl's company, she also found him more than a little unsettling, and she wasn't certain how repeated visits with the gentleman would affect her concentration. Truth to tell, it might be altogether dangerous to be too often in this man's company, hence she amended, "It may prove rather tedious."

"I'm certain I'll survive. Perhaps you shall even make a believer of me."

"Oh, no, my lord, I would never try to change you. No one save yourself can do that and of your own free will."

Her statement was as comforting as it was unexpected. Recalling Max's warning about the female penchant for reformation, he couldn't help being drawn toward this young woman who possessed such a rational outlook on life. What a logical creature she was, and out of the blue he found himself speculating whether or not his kiss had ruffled Lady Sarah. Well, he decided, the only way to find out would be to kiss her again, and he determined to do so at the next available opportunity.

5

I F IT WAS possible for two perfectly sensible adults
to transform into a pair of tattlemongers in a peri-
od of less than twenty-four hours the behavior of
Lady Ophelia and Mr. Carysfort proved the point.
No sooner had their respective younger relatives
departed for the Countess of Mornington's garden
than the couple was engaged in an avid gossip.

They were in the extensive brick and glass structure which housed the celebrated Great Vine, the
horticultural wonder that had been planted in 1769
and whose principal stem had achieved a length of
over one hundred feet. In the autumn fruitful season, some three thousand clusters of purple-black
Hamburgh grapes presented a beautiful curiosity
to the sightseers who toured the palace gardens.
In May, the gardener, as a means of making his
spring pruning easier, encouraged the grace-and-

favor residents to clip sprigs of vine, and it was this activity in which Lady Ophelia was engaged. The bright green leaves would make a perfect bed for the arrangement of rich scarlet colored roses she planned to display in her drawing room.

"Sarah was unusually preoccupied this morning," Lady Ophelia reported as she snipped several green lengths and dropped them into the rush basket which Mr. Carysfort was carrying for her. "She scarcely touched her chocolate, and although I assumed it was owing to the ruined vigil, I'm sure something else is preying upon her mind."

"It must have been the kiss," was Mr. Carysfort's deceptively casual reply.

"The what?" Lady Ophelia's busy hands stilled, and she looked up from her work.

"He kissed her."

"He? Who? What in heaven's name are you talking about, Max?"

"Didn't Sarah tell you about the gentleman in the Clock Court?"

"Well, yes, but she didn't say anything about a kiss. Besides how do you know what happened?"

"It was Radnor."

"Your nephew's here?"

"Indeed, he's come to stay for awhile."

"And he *kissed* Sarah?" Lady Ophelia imagined she sounded rather simple-minded, but she was finding this intelligence difficult to comprehend.

"Apparently so."

"I suppose I ought to feel some sense of motherly outrage that a stranger dared to take such a liberty with Sarah, but, truth to tell, I don't. A kiss, you say. And it was Lord Radnor." Lady Ophelia pondered this for a moment. "Do you think he's in love?"

Mr. Carysfort laughed. "So soon? Not likely. Besides for Radnor, a stolen kiss, outrageous though it may be, is quite true to form. It's when a gentleman acts out of character that his behavior can be considered a sign of love."

"You say that as if it were a hard and fast rule."

"Actually, I made it up."

"Based on your own behavior?" Lady Ophelia gave Mr. Carysfort a gentle smile. "Well, it does sound convincing. I wonder if the same holds true for women."

"Well, does it?"

Lady Ophelia recalled Sarah's response to her question as to whether or not the gentleman had been good-looking. *I didn't notice.* The tall, blue-eyed and ebony-haired Carysfort men were known for their powerful and undeniably masculine good looks, and it would be impossible for any woman not to notice the Earl of Radnor, especially Sarah, who had trained her eye to take in even the smallest detail. A rush of girlish excitement assailed Lady Ophelia at the implication of Sarah's uncharacteristic behavior. "As you say, it's probably too soon for them to truly be in love, but I suspect there's the basis of an attraction which might lead to something more. Oh, Max, this is the best thing that could have happened. It may be the solution to our little problem," she said with ingenious understatement.

"That was exactly my thought."

"Oh, I do wish I could have been there last night."

Mr. Carysfort chuckled. "While you may wish to have been in the Clock Court last evening, I'd much rather be in Lady Mornington's garden as we speak."

"You would?"

"Of course. I sent Radnor off to pay his respects to Lady Mornington." He sounded extremely pleased with his cleverness. "It's been quite some time since he went off."

"Perhaps they're at one another's throats. Sarah's not one to put up with the least bit of arrogance from anyone." There was more than a touch of worry in Lady Ophelia's voice.

"Not likely. He thought her hair was—and I quote—glorious," came his offhand remark.

"Max, you're holding out on me. Kisses. Admiring remarks. What else did Lord Radnor say?"

"That Sarah was the most outspoken female he'd ever encountered. She called him a pompous peacock."

"Oh, that's not good." Lady Ophelia frowned.

"It may have been the best thing to happen. I don't believe Beverly's ever encountered a young lady who didn't trip over herself to get him to look her way. Sarah apparently was distinctly unimpressed by my nephew, therefore proving herself to be one of a kind. There was a certain fascination in his voice when he talked about her. No doubt about it, she's intrigued him. Now tell me what did Sarah say about him?"

"Not much. She didn't even give the slightest hint that he'd kissed her, but I think that omission speaks volumes."

He nodded in agreement. "I do believe they're

suited. They're both quick witted and enjoy the out-of-doors."

With much enthusiasm, Lady Ophelia put in, "And if my memory of Lord Radnor serves me well, I believe they both own a deplorable lack of interest in the opera. Didn't you once say he had a secret penchant for architectural history? Sarah would appreciate that. Why, just imagine, he might even come to share her fondness for the palace."

"You're quite right. The trick is to make them see everything they own in common."

"Should we formulate a plan?" she asked, suddenly queasy with the thought that she might do anything manipulative behind Sarah's back.

"Not yet. Let's wait and see how things develop on their own. We must be very careful, y'know," Mr. Carysfort cautioned. "The very reason Beverly's come to stay at the palace is to escape the ploys of marriage-minded young ladies, and I doubt there's any wile to which my nephew hasn't been subjected."

"Then we must simply begin with proximity." Lady Ophelia, no longer distracted, recommenced snipping at the vine. Earlier this morning, she'd been in a fret about Sarah's future, now it seemed as if a solution, needing just the tiniest bit of prodding, was on the horizon. She gave an optimistic smile as she set several curling lengths of greenery in the basket. "As you and I have the excuse of planning our wedding we shall contrive to have the four of us together on every possible occasion. Given those circumstances, neither of them should be in the least bit suspicious."

So it was that Lady Sarah and the Earl of Radnor

found themselves in one another's company once if not twice each day. Following that encounter in the Countess of Mornington's garden and subsequent impromptu tour of the palace gardens, there was tea with Mr. Carysfort and Lady Ophelia. The next day, being Wednesday, it was the ladies' weekly outing to the church yard in the nearby village of Teddington, tea again, and then a moonlight stroll down the Broad Walk. Thursday, they engaged in a game of early morning tennis in the enclosed court which had been constructed for the pleasure of Henry the Eighth. And Friday, while they managed to elude Mr. Carysfort and Lady Ophelia, they were together once more as this was the day Sarah had arranged to visit the Old Court House and the earl tagged along.

The interview with the cook had concluded, and Sarah, who had taken copious notes, placed her papers into a canvas satchel which she handed to the earl. After thanking Lady MacGregor for allowing them to intrude upon her household, Lady Sarah and the earl departed the pretty house to walk along the quay that edged the Thames.

Lord Radnor was the first to speak. "If I didn't know Uncle Max as well as I do, I'd swear some clever matchmaking was at work here."

"That's ridiculous," was Sarah's instant reply. "I'm quite beyond the age of hunting for a husband, and Aunt Ophelia has never been the sort to cast about for a match for me." Sarah had hardly uttered that final syllable when she recalled her conversation with Lady Ophelia the morning after the musicale, and although she didn't voice it aloud she knew a momentary suspicion of her own. She was prompted to inquire, "Why would you say such a thing?"

"We seem to be thrown together quite a bit."

"Oh, that's easy enough to explain," she said with some relief. "You obviously don't know as much about Mr. Carysfort as you thought. We quite live in one another's pockets here. Verily, I often think of Mr. Carysfort as my uncle."

Lord Radnor considered this explanation and found it lacking. "Don't you think it peculiar that they've managed to send us off unchaperoned on more than one occasion?"

Sarah paused and tilted her head sideways to peek up at the earl from beneath the brim of her straw bonnet. Her violet eyes danced with amusement, and she laughed. It was a light tinkling sound that reminded the earl of a summer breeze teasing the treetops. Her laughter continued, and this time, he did not accuse her of behaving like a serving wench. This time, a warm smile suffused his features, for again her laughter was that gentle companionable sound of which he was growing fond.

"My dear, sir," she began on the end of her laughter. "There are myriad reasons why the question of a chaperone is wholly irrelevant. First, I'm hardly of an age to need one. Second, the opinions of society do not matter to me. I'm no green girl to tremble at the prospect of being denied a voucher to Almack's. Verily, most ladies fear the censure of Society will harm their chances for marriage, but as I harbor no aspirations in that quarter, I have nothing to fear."

"Yes, I see your point," said the earl, who was suddenly and unaccountably struck by the fact that

Lady Sarah's position on marriage seemed to be a terrible waste. Staring down at her delicate upturned face, he took in her glowing pink cheeks and pretty features, particularly those naturally red lips that formed a perfect bow, and he could not help thinking that such a singular young lady would make some fortunate gentleman a most unique wife. "But don't you intend to marry?"

"Perish the thought," was her instant rejoinder.

"But I thought that was the dearest ambition of all young ladies."

"Marriage is for women who must define themselves in terms of a relationship to a man rather than in terms of themselves and their own accomplishments. First, they are daughters, then wives, and then mothers to heirs. My years as a daughter were few, and although I dearly loved my father his death forced me to think of myself as a separate entity. I know who I am and have done much with my few years, and most important of all, I can imagine many more years of accomplishment without a man's guidance or intervention."

The earl shook his head in astonishment. "I've never known anyone like you before."

"Not a female, I'd wager, but certainly, your male friends must share similar views. How about yourself, my lord? Why haven't you married?"

For the first time, the Earl of Radnor was at a loss for words. How could he tell Lady Sarah there was nothing marriage offered him that he didn't already enjoy? Even a lady as broad-minded as Lady Sarah would find offense with such a remark. He skirted the whole truth. "Like yourself my life is quite full the way it is. The only sort of marriage I would ever consider is one of convenience to ensure an heir, and sooner or later I will have to do just that. But even then, mind you, I won't expect to be shackled to the lady. Whomever I marry must see eye to eye with me on that matter, for I would expect each of us to go our separate ways."

"That sounds most sensible," Sarah said as she resumed strolling along the quay. A gust of wind blew off the Thames, tugging at her bonnet, and without giving it a second thought, she took off the hat and carried it like a reticule by its velvet ribbons.

Again, the earl was astounded, not so much by the impropriety of such an action, but by the fact that he had always assumed ladies, especially ladies of Quality, loathed even the most minuscule exposure to the elements. "The sun doesn't bother you, Lady Sarah?"

"No, my lord, I adore the out-of-doors." Once more she laughed, and once more the earl found himself feeling most comfortable with Lady Sarah.

Here, for the first time, Lord Radnor had found a young lady who had no designs upon him as a man, a young lady with whom—and this was a startling idea—he might become friends. But the appeal of this discovery was short-lived when coupled with the fact that he considered Lady Sarah a most kissable young lady. If he wished to be her friend that sort of desire was entirely out of place. Moreover, and this was, in truth, what disturbed him the most about his unusual train of thoughts, it was distinctly unsettling to look at the desirable Lady Sarah and realize that apparently she didn't reciprocate his sentiments.

6

THE MOST CHARITABLE thing to be said about Miss Camilla Burges Watson was that she was only slightly less unappealing than her twin sister Pamela. Both girls had lumpy figures, doughy complexions, and the variety of long questing noses associated with Latin tutors. It was not, however, their lack of physical attributes that made them unbecoming—for there were many young ladies who were equally as plain but whose sweetness of disposition overcame that unattractiveness—rather it was their manner of speech. The Burges Watson twins giggled incessantly, spoke in affected high-pitched lisps, and every third or fourth statement from their mouths was modified with, "Mama says."

Their personalities were no better. They were petty, vain and self-centered, and the only sympathetic point in their favor was that having grown up under their mama's thumb they could not be blamed for their repellent behavior.

Mrs. Burges Watson, the daughter of a West End butcher, while having managed to marry the youngest son of the Marquess of Maryborough had not managed to divest herself of numerous plebeian habits such as making an intentional public spectacle of herself and her daughters.

As predictable as it was that every Sunday morning the Reverend Wellesley would invoke at least one Biblical verse on the Seventh Commandment, it was equally as predictable that Mrs. Burges Watson would arrive at the Chapel Royal at the precise moment necessary to parade her daughters down the aisle no more than three feet behind the processional entrance of the good chaplain and his acolytes.

This Sunday morning was no different. Dressed in identical Angoulême walking costumes, the Burges Watson twins sashayed down the aisle, distinguishable from one another only by the fact that Mrs. Burges Watson always insisted that Camilla wear hues of insipid pale pink, while Pamela wore shades of pale green. Most of the residents of Hampton Court ignored this weekly display, but there were always enough visitors for Sunday services, particularly eligible male visitors, to warrant a repeat performance.

Sarah, who was seated in the Clement-Brooke family pew in the right transept at the front of the chapel, observed several gaping visitors. Disapproval mingled with revulsion was evident upon many a face, and wishing to measure the earl's reaction, she glanced his way.

It had only been five days since the earl had arrived at Hampton Court, yet in many ways it was as if they had known one another forever, and without hearing him speak Sarah knew why he was staring at her with such alarm. Every horrified line upon his face was asking, "Are those the dreaded twins?"

Sarah inclined her head a fraction of an inch to indicate an affirmative reply the result of which did nothing to erase the aversion upon his countenance.

"Duty to the Crown. What young gentleman did not hear those very words time and again during his public school career?" It was the Reverend Wellesley, and Sarah turned away from the earl to listen to the sermon. This morning, the subject was the virtue of loyalty to country, King and God, and Wellesley concluded with a request for the congregation's prayers for the allied army on the Continent. "Let us pray for the whole state of Christ's Church."

The communion service was more than half-way over, and as the congregation filed to the altar to receive the host Sarah's thoughts drifted to matters less holy. She was cogitating on the next phase of her investigation into the suspicious noises at the Old Court House by the river when a high-pitched female squeal drew her attention back to the row of pews where the earl was seated.

The origin of the squeal was Camilla Burges Watson, and she had collapsed in a swoon. But this was no regular swoon. By some miracle Miss Burges Watson had managed to faint directly into the lap of the Earl of Radnor, and as she was no dainty creature her form also leaned heavily upon Mr. Carysfort.

After several unsuccessful attempts to push the young woman off his shoulder, Mr. Carysfort spoke in an agitated over-loud whisper, "Well, take her out of here, man. What are you waiting for? Get her a breath of fresh air."

The earl was scarcely visible beneath a pile of salmon pink taffeta topped with a hat trimmed with fleur-de-lis, its brim edged in floss silk and a white ostrich feather dangling to one side. None too steadily, the earl stood and half-carried, half-hauled the young woman from the chapel to the nearest courtyard. Mr. Carysfort straightened his neck cloth and remained seated; oddly, neither Mrs. Burges Watson nor her other daughter made a move to see if Camilla was all right.

Something was not right here, and although Sarah was not sure what that something could be, she found herself whispering, "Excuse me, Aunt Ophelia, I must go and see if Camilla is all right."

Normally, Lady Ophelia would have questioned Sarah's interest in one of the Burges Watson twins. It wasn't that Sarah was uncaring, but rather that she owned little patience for either girl and tended to avoid their company whenever she politely could. Lady Ophelia, however, had a fairly good notion of why Camilla had fainted, and in this instance, Sarah's concern was most providential. Hence, she encouraged, "Yes, my dear, do go and see if you can assist the poor child."

Outside in the Chapel Court Sarah did not see the earl nor his damsel in distress, but she could hear Camilla's high-pitched lisp.

"The sunlight, my lord, 'tis far too bright. Mama says it isn't healthy for a young lady. Oh, please, sir, you must shelter me from it lest I faint again," she pleaded with much dramatic skill.

Sarah hurried around a corner toward Camilla's voice and came upon them in a shady recess of the court. The earl was attempting to set the girl upon her feet, but the young lady would not loose her arms from about his neck.

"Camilla, you must let go of his lordship or else you shall both land in a heap upon the ground." Sarah spoke more sharply than she intended.

At the sight of Sarah dismay burst upon Camilla's face, her gaze narrowed and the look she cast upon Sarah was as frigid as a mid-winter gale, all of which caused Sarah to arrive at the realization that landing in a compromising heap had, in truth, been Camilla's primary objective.

"Lady Sarah, what are you doing here?" she lisped.

"I came to see if you were all right," Sarah explained, impatience beginning to lace her words. "Apparently, your mother cares little for your health or the dictums of propriety, and I thought I might offer assistance. However, if the strength of your grip about his lordship's neck is any indication of your health, I'd say you were fit as a fiddle."

Camilla let go, and, for a second, it appeared Miss Burges Watson might pitch a scene, then she composed herself.

"Thank you, Lady Sarah. It was most considerate of you to be concerned," she said in a simpering tone of voice. She curtsied to the earl and cooed, "And thank you, sir. Had you not caught me I would certainly have sustained a most dreadful head injury. Mama would say it was most heroic of you, and I'd agree." She giggled.

"You must be more careful in the future." The Earl of Radnor projected the same haughty persona as when he had encountered Sarah in the Clock Court. "I'm sure the Reverend Wellesley would not take offense to your slipping outside for a breath of fresh air should you ever feel faint again. A discreet exit would be preferable to having a repeat of such a scene in his chapel."

"Yes, of course, you're very wise, my lord. Of course, I shall follow your advice." Fluttering her eyelashes with the most horrendous speed, she looked up at him and giggled some more.

"Camilla, where are you?" It was Mrs. Burges Watson. As if reciting lines from a script, she called out, "You should not be alone with a gentleman, Camilla. Where are you? Answer this instant, my dear."

"We are here, ma'am," supplied the earl.

The mother bustled around the corner, followed on her heels by a leering Pamela. Both were brought up short at the sight of Sarah.

"Lady Sarah!"

"Yes, it's I, and you can set your concerns aside, for your daughter has not been unchaperoned. Both her health and reputation are in immaculate form."

"Ah, yes, well, thank you, Lady Sarah, and you, too, my lord, for catching my daughter, who apparently does not have the sense of a tulip bulb." She curtsied. "You must allow me to introduce myself.

I am Mrs. Burges Watson and these are my daughters, Camilla and Pamela."

Pamela took this as her cue to step forward, perform a curtsy and giggle. The earl executed the necessary bow before each female and repeated his earlier advice for Camilla to Mrs. Burges Watson, who thanked him, and then commenced a recitation of her family situation.

"We are residents here at the palace, my lord. My good husband, Lord bless his soul, was a calvary officer in the Life Guards, y'know, and while my father-in-law did offer us accommodations in the dower house at Maryborough Hall, Chester is such a long way off, and we thought this arrangement much more to our liking. What with two eligible daughters who wish to be near all the Season's festivities living in grace and favour is much more convenient. Don't you agree?"

The purpose behind this monologue was obviously to inform the earl of her social status and of the availability of Camilla and Pamela. It was, however, so appallingly ill-bred that Sarah knew a pang of sympathy for the girls.

Mrs. Burges Watson concluded, "Of course, we must repay you, my lord, for your gallantry. Perhaps you'll consent to join us for tea one day this week."

"I should be delighted," he replied without a blink.

Sarah was shocked by his acceptance, but not nearly as dumbfounded as when he added: "Of course, I shall only visit, if Lady Sarah agrees to come along, for she, too, was most helpful in this situation."

Mrs. Burges Watson's response was restrained. "That would be fine, my lord. Shall we say Wednesday?"

"Yes, Wednesday would suit. Thank you."

Mrs. Burges Watson gave a frosty smile, then glared at Camilla, who had proven herself a gross failure at the fine art of subterfuge. "Come along, my dears."

"Yes, Mama," the twins lisped in unison.

The three Burges Watson females retreated. They were barely out of earshot before Sarah turned upon the earl.

"Why didn't you refuse her invitation?" She didn't bother to wait for his reply, but hurried on, "Besides which you had no right to include me in that invitation. Not only was it in poor taste to impose me upon Mrs. Burges Watson, but you've no right to manage my life in such a high-handed fashion."

The earl was unperturbed by Sarah's reprimand. "If I have to endure a tea with those women, you must as well, for none of this would have come to pass, if you hadn't been derelict in your duty."

"What in the world are you talking about?" She pinned him with her most annoyed look.

"I thought you were going to warn me."

"But I knew nothing of their plans. And I must say that until I saw Camilla clinging to your neck like a vine, I didn't have the foggiest notion what was afoot. I'm not terribly knowledgeable in such devious matters, y'know."

"Well, now you see how it is."

"And you do have my sympathies. But why did you accept their invitation in the first place? That doesn't make sense to me."

"It makes a great deal of sense, if one accepts that the best way to defeat one's enemy is to know one's enemy. It's my diffuse and confuse strategy. By accepting their invitation I put a halt, albeit temporary, to their ploys, for as long as they believe they have my attention they will refrain from such drastic measures to attain it."

"There must be an easier way than having to visit the dragon—as it were—in its lair." In her mind's eye, Sarah envisioned a picture of the earl beset by fawning Burges Watson females, this one pressing a platter of scones upon him, that one adding far too much sugar to his tea. Her lower lip began to tremble with impending laughter, and she tried to disguise a widening grin with one gloved hand.

The earl saw Sarah's attempt to control her mounting amusement, and as if reading the direction of her thoughts he grinned. "Yes, it's always quite a ghastly production," he drawled in a voice heavy with feigned weariness, and in the next instant, they both yielded to unbridled laughter.

At length, Sarah took a deep breath. "We should not carry on so, my lord. It's quite heartless to find humor at someone else's expense."

"Heartless it may be, but I must or else these incessant assaults on my person would drive me to Bedlam. I don't consider it amusing to perpetually find myself on the verge of tumbling into one scandal broth or another, and if I don't make light of it, I should be tense and blue-deviled every moment of every day."

"Stated that way it's understandable why you require such a release. The situation is, indeed, desperate. Truth to tell, you're quite doomed, my lord," she teased. "Your future is a bleak one. It's either madness or marriage, but which might be the lesser evil I can't say."

He laughed anew, and she joined in, their merriment building to such heights that a tear escaped Sarah's eye. When their laughter died down, Sarah took another steadying breath, and Radnor lifted a hand to brush the tear from her cheek.

His touch was quick, the backside of his fingers gently brushing her cheek in an upward motion, but not so brief that Sarah's heart didn't somersault and her breath catch in her throat as their eyes met and held.

Of a sudden, the memory of that kiss in the Clock Court returned to Sarah with such impact that her lips began to tingle. Her tongue darted out to moisten her lips, the breath in her throat released, and her chest rose and fell as she glanced from his eyes to his full mouth and then back to his eyes. She could tell he, too, was thinking about it by the way his eyes looked downward to focus upon her mouth in such a fashion that it seemed as if he were touching her. Several moments passed before his gaze lifted, and once more violet eyes locked with Aegean blue.

It was a long and loaded moment. Everything around Sarah diminished in size and sound until she was aware of nothing but the earl's tall powerful form hovering above her; she focused on nothing but his parted lips. The only sound she heard was the amplified beating of her heart, so loud she was certain even Lord Radnor could hear its furious pounding.

It seemed an eternity elapsed before he spoke. "You have the most remarkable eyes, my lady," he murmured in a husky voice that made Sarah shiver despite the noonday warmth. He stepped closer, blocking out the sun, his steady gaze holding hers as he raised a hand toward her face.

It was a fairy tale moment. The kind that Sarah had only overheard other girls talk about, and despite her lack of experience in such matters, Sarah was certain that the earl was going to kiss her again. It was a notion that held a surprising appeal, and thus, she wasn't sure why she broke the spell by saying, "Laughter is a wonderful curative, isn't it, my lord? I don't know the last time I laughed so hard."

Radnor's raised hand fell to his side, and there was a momentary flash of disappointment upon his face. "It feels good, doesn't it?"

"Yes." She changed the subject. "I don't know how you've survived this far. Even though you may have managed to avoid madness, it's nothing short of miraculous that you've eluded matrimony."

"It's been a hardship."

"Faith, sir, I believe you need a bodyguard." Sarah's violet eyes sparkled.

A roguish grin turned up at the corners of Lord Radnor's full mouth. He reflected aloud, "A bodyguard. Yes, that's something I must consider." Then he offered his arm, and she accepted his escort as they headed back to Mr. Carysfort's suite for luncheon.

7

AT THREE O'CLOCK the following afternoon, the Countess of Mornington paid a call upon Lady Ophelia. Something of great importance was preying upon the elderly lady's mind. For several days, she'd been intrigued by the notion that Lady Sarah was the right young woman to put a stop to the Earl of Radnor's bachelor days. Romance had been lurking below the surface in her garden last week, she was certain of it. But the dreadful incident involving that Burges Watson creature had caused the countess to pass a sleepless night, her head inundated with worries that some harpy might lure the earl into the parson's mousetrap before Lady Sarah came to her senses, and this morning, Lady Mornington was determined to do something about the matter.

The countess and Lady Ophelia were seated upon

the gilt beechwood sofa in Lady Ophelia's drawing room. A pitcher of tart lemonade, one of Sarah's favorite treats, and iced glasses with sprigs of fresh mint rested upon a nearby table. In the sunny window seat on the other side of the drawing room, Sarah was engaged in conversation with Miss Eugenia Wellesley, Lady Mornington's great-granddaughter, who was recently betrothed to Viscount Strabane and had that morning arrived from the Wellesley family seat north of Dublin to prepare for her wedding.

"Now tell me, Lady Ophelia, what are you going to do about Lady Sarah?" The countess's question fell upon the drawing room with the impact of a French artillery bombardment.

Lady Ophelia's mouth opened and closed several times like a haddock in its final throes upon the fishmonger's cart. At length, she managed to utter something that sounded like "Aaargh." In an uncomfortable gesture, Miss Wellesley raised a hand behind which she blushed with the proper measure of embarrassment. Sarah, for her part, was, contrary to normal expectation, merely amused by all of this. She enjoyed another sip of lemonade before she addressed Miss Wellesley in a whisper, "I do wish Lady Mornington wouldn't talk about me as if I were the village idiot."

"My great-grandmother can be prodigiously perturbing." Miss Wellesley, relieved that Sarah was not offended by her elder relative's outspoken query, gave Sarah a conspiratorial wink and raised her voice, "Pray ma'am, I could not help overhearing what you said to Lady Ophelia. Is there something wrong with Lady Sarah's health?"

"Her aunt is soon to be married to Mr. Carysfort," said Lady Mornington as if that statement alone was sufficient explanation, then she leveled her lorgnette upon Sarah. "What will you do when Lady Ophelia is married?"

"I had not given it much thought, ma'am, but now that you raise the subject I believe I should like to visit my brother Simon in Palestine."

"Egad, child, you mustn't entertain such a farrago of nonsense." The countess gave voice to the dismay that was etched upon Lady Ophelia's face.

"But, ma'am, I haven't seen my brother in more than five years," Sarah said. "Nor have I travelled in many more years than that, and of late, I find his letters quite frustrating. I miss the excitement and sounds and colors of the East and wish to experience it all for myself."

"You never mentioned this to me," Lady Ophelia responded. "I had no idea you wished to leave England."

"Fustian, Lady Ophelia, it's nothing but fustian. Heed the advice of one who has lived longer and knows best. You mustn't take any of it seriously. If Sarah desires to see her brother, he can come home." The countess pointed her lorgnette in Sarah's direction. "It's high time *you* were settled."

"Excuse me, ma'am?" Sarah, who had always considered the Countess of Mornington a staunch ally in matters of feminine independence, wondered if she had misunderstood the lady.

"Settled," repeated Lady Mornington, then she clarified, "as in married."

Now it was Sarah's turn to behave like a netted salmon. Indeed, so great was her amazement that she did not notice the approving little nod and thankful smile her aunt bestowed upon Lady Mornington.

"You may believe otherwise, but arrangements won't be the same once Lady Ophelia is wed, and you must begin thinking about your own life, my dear."

"Faith, ma'am, that is my intention." Sarah sat a bit straighter and her fingers tightened about her lemonade glass as she schooled her voice to disguise her indignation. A moment ago, this conversation was somewhat amusing, now, however, it was touching upon threatening. While Sarah, as a general rule, did not mind guidance from Lady Mornington, she did not appreciate anyone acting as if they had a right to make decisions in her behalf. "Please, don't think me rude to contradict you, ma'am, but I do have plans for my own life, and they don't include being shackled to a gentleman for no other reason than a necessity of timing."

The countess lowered her lorgnette and smiled. "Dear Sarah, I don't think you rude. Outspoken and opinionated, yes. No, you're not rude, my dear, but you are sadly misguided about the state of matrimony. You speak as if marriage were tantamount to deportation to Botany Bay, but I assure you it doesn't have to be that way."

"Indeed, Lady Sarah, my great-grandmother is correct," Miss Wellesley gave her whole-hearted endorsement. "Permit me to say that once I held fast to a similar belief and was determined never to wed. You see, I own the less than ladylike habit of donating my time and purse money to the local bettering society for orphans. And although my parents gave me the usual come-out, it did nothing to change my determination to help those less fortunate than myself. Every gentleman I encountered disdained my charitable endeavors, and I did not wish to marry, for I feared those gentlemen would expect me to give it up. Then I met Viscount Strabane." She blushed prettily. "Christian does not circulate on the front line of fashion, nor is he a Corinthian or Man About Town, but he respects my involvement with the bettering society. He is my friend and my best supporter, and I know that to marry Christian will only make my work more rewarding. You must not think of marriage as some dire variety of penal sentence, but rather as a means to have a companion and confidant for life, in particular someone who might encourage you and love you all the more because you are not like everyone else."

"I had not thought of it like that," said Sarah, arriving at the expected conclusion that Miss Wellesley's description of marriage was rather beautiful. But owing to the recent changes in Aunt Ophelia's outlook regarding her social life, Sarah did not express this opinion. She did not wish to plant any more bees in her aunt's bonnet. The safest thing to say was, "But I can think of no one who would fit that bill for me."

"Then you must get about more in Society. You will never meet anyone, if you don't enlarge your circle of acquaintances," said Miss Wellesley.

"That is precisely what I've been telling my niece," Lady Ophelia said in ardent accord. What a remarkable bit of good fortune that the Countess of Mornington had decided to meddle in Sarah's affairs and that the marriage-smitten Miss Wellesley had come to call. This was bound to have a favorable influence upon her efforts to effect a match between the Earl of Radnor and Sarah.

The countess gave Lady Ophelia an approving pat upon the forearm. "You remain as wise as I've always thought. The Season is upon us, and you must accept every invitation which comes your way. If need be, you and Lady Sarah should take temporary residence in Town. What engagements have you on your calendar?"

"We begin with the Anglesea ball."

"Excellent. And what about Lady Russborough's turtle dinner? Are you attending?"

"I received an invitation today, but we had not discussed it yet."

"Pray, Lady Ophelia, what is there to discuss? Of course, you'll both attend. Eugenia's father is arranging for carriages to take us to Town the evening of the ball, and you shall ride with us," Lady Mornington pronounced in a take charge sort of tenor.

"That is most kind of you, Lady Mornington."

"Not kind, merely practical. And while we're at it we'll have that modiste Madame Tizou—who I hear from Lady Cotton's sister is all the rage—measure Sarah for a new ball gown. Eugenia needs some new dresses, and we shall see to it that both young ladies are elegantly attired."

Miss Wellesley's face brightened, and she expressed great appreciation at the prospect of a new ball gown. She confided in Sarah, "I know it's prodigiously frivolous of me, but I own the most dreadful weakness when it comes to dancing frocks. Even in Dublin Madame Tizou's reputation is highly acclaimed. Tell me, Lady Sarah, have you any dresses from her needle?"

"No," Sarah said in a preoccupied tone. Of a sudden, Sarah was a tad queasy, and she set her lemonade glass aside. She had always been able to maintain a level-headed poise during the most frightening vigils, thus it was deeply unsettling to find herself shaken by an innocent discussion of ball gowns.

"Oh, aren't we both the most fortunate young ladies? I do hope I'll be able to wear something other than white or pale yellow. I've always had a fondness for magenta velvet. What is your preference, Lady Sarah? Amethyst silk would be splendid with your eyes, y'know. Oh, I can't wait to select my new ball gown, can you?"

"No," came another reticent reply from Sarah, who had no idea what she had said as she struggled to retain an outwardly calm demeanor. A *new* ball gown? The notion was wholly alien to Sarah. Having never needed one, she did not own a ball gown, and her formal wardrobe was limited to an unadorned and out-dated Empire style gown of ecru India muslin which had always suited her needs. Although Sarah knew it was foolish to allow the mention of lilac silk to weigh heavily upon her mind, she could not quash the onset of her worries.

In the past, Sarah had always believed she controlled her life, but she was beginning to think that this was not the case. Whether or not she wished a ball gown or to attend any of those parties was of no account; Aunt Ophelia and Lady Mornington were acting as if she were a debutante embarking upon her first Season rather than a grown woman with mature interests that had nothing to do with turtle dinners and lilac silk. Sarah gave a tired sigh. There had been a lot of changes in the past week beginning with the arrival of the Earl of Radnor. Verily, it seemed as if months, instead of a mere sennight, had passed since the earl had come to Hampton Court, and she wasn't quite sure what that meant.

One thing was certain. Sarah couldn't shake off the feeling that something was going to happen. It was that same feeling she often sensed when on a ghost vigil, and she knew she needed to be on her guard.

8

"ZEUS AND MINERVA! Don't tell me it's Wednesday already," Lady Sarah exclaimed upon learning the Earl of Radnor was waiting to escort her to Mrs. Burges Watson's apartment. "Oh, Aunt Ophelia, look at this. I can't possibly go anywhere."

She motioned about the drawing room that was littered with dozens of history books, newspaper clippings, several issues of the *Philosophical Transactions* of the Royal Society, and voluminous correspondence from the physicist, Thomas Young, who had taken time from the decipherment of the Rosetta Stone to share his theories on light emanation and the perception of color. A vigil in the Old Court House had been scheduled in three days' time. This confusion was preparatory to that event. Sarah needed to review the history of the house and its former occupants, to familiarize herself with its architectural design, and to become acquainted with the latest publications on the science of light and sound, for such matters—though never intended to apply to the supernatural—might prove invaluable to her investigation.

Sarah's mind was a jumble of facts and dates and complex scientific theorems. Not only had she managed to lose total track of time, she had completely forgotten about the earl and their visit to Mrs. Burges Watson and her daughters.

A mere fortnight ago, Lady Ophelia would have been immeasurably pleased to see Sarah absorbed in her work. Today, however, she was more than a little annoyed. It was all well and good for the girl not to have tripped over her hems to impress Radnor when they had first met, but it was quite another matter to forget about him altogether. While the former may have engendered a certain intrigue on the part of the earl for Sarah, the latter was bound to cause the gentleman to experience distinct offense and become displeased with, if not disinterested in, Sarah. And that must not be allowed to happen.

"Your work can wait, Sarah. The Old Court House has been standing for well over a century and shall remain another week or two at least. The earl, however, must soon depart, if he is to arrive at Mrs. Burges Watson's on time, and you must hurry, if you don't wish to make him late."

This was the last thing Sarah expected to hear from Aunt Ophelia. Never before had her aunt considered anything more important than their work. Verily, Aunt Ophelia had even been known to employ tiny white lies when it was necessary to cancel a social engagement or turn away a visitor

because of a project. This change in attitude was
most peculiar, and the best that Sarah could manage
to utter was a weak, "But—," before Lady Ophelia
plunged onward in her speech.

"No, there can be absolutely no excuses, this
time, my dear. You must hurry to your room to
change." The younger woman was wearing a simple dress that was several years out of fashion, and
her hair was a hopeless mass of curls that had
fallen free of a chignon pinned with an antique bod-
kin. "Don't give a second thought to these things.
You've been reading since sunrise, and the break
will do you good."

"Are you feeling yourself, Aunt Ophelia?" Sarah
was unable to prevent herself from asking, for Lady
Ophelia had never suggested that she change clothes
in the middle of the day. Although it might be the
accepted practice in Town, the idea was, to Sarah's
mind, a preposterous waste of time.

"Why ever would you wonder such a thing?"
Lady Ophelia, who knew very well why Sarah
had proffered such a query, feigned ignorance.
She picked up several books, closed them and
set them on a nearby table. "Oh, perhaps, I'm a
tad overwhelmed with the details for the wedding. Darling Max wishes to have a large affair
at St. George's, y'know, and every Carysfort that
can walk—including the dowager countess—shall
descend on the metropolis and expect to be fed,
housed and entertained. But aside from all that,
yes, I'm feeling myself. Now do hurry and put
away those notes so you can change, and perhaps,
we can do *something* with your hair."

"I think Lady Sarah looks charming just the way

she is." The smooth male voice came from the doorway, and the ladies turned to see the Earl of Radnor
standing upon the threshold. His gaze was riveted
to the sight of Lady Sarah seated upon an Agras
prayer carpet, her skirt in a purplish shade of blue
fanned out about her like the petals of a gillyflower,
and the bright afternoon sun shimmering off her
glorious flaxen hair. He had not seen her since
Sunday luncheon—having made the grave error of
attending a boxing match the following day and
engaging in a lengthy celebration with some cronies
which required he spend Tuesday recuperating from
his folly—and he was struck by the realization that
Lady Sarah, in all her natural and unsophisticated
splendor, became more breathtaking each time he
saw her.

"Oh, hallo, Lord Radnor," said Sarah. The gentle
pink color in her cheeks deepened, for while she
was not dismayed to have been discovered sitting
on the floor with her attention focused on matters
academic, she was quite unaccustomed to receiving
compliments from a gentleman. Also she could not
deny the peculiar fluttering in her mid-section since
he had entered the room.

"I didn't hear you trying to cry off, did I?" the
earl asked as he crossed the drawing room and
went to stand on the other side of a pile of architectural renderings. It was the closest he could get
to Lady Sarah, and he executed a tidy bow to each
of the ladies.

"It's not that I was trying to avoid your company,
sir," came Sarah's ingenuous response. Her violet
eyes sparkled with delight, for despite the demands
of her work she was pleased to see this amusing

gentleman with whom she could easily converse. "It's rather that I've too much work and too little time. Late last evening, I received a missive from Lady MacGregor informing me that she and the major will be visiting their son in Sussex. While they're gone I can have free access to the Old Court House."

"Can I help?" he offered.

"Short of calling off this excursion to Mrs. Burges Watson I don't see how."

Lady Ophelia flashed Sarah a quick look that bespoke annoyance, then bestowed a bright smile upon the earl. The gentleman's offer was a golden opportunity for her matchmaking efforts, and she wasn't going to let it be rejected. "Your offer is most generous, Lord Radnor, and as you were present for the initial interview, I think including you in the investigative endeavor from beginning to end is a superlative notion. Indeed, your offer couldn't have come at a more provident time, for I find myself overwhelmed with wedding plans and unable to offer Sarah the assistance she requires."

Sarah studied her aunt. What was wrong with her today? Allowing the earl to accompany her on a preliminary interview and a vigil or two was one thing, but including him in an entire project could become a hindrance. Aunt Ophelia appeared healthy, but why was she acting in such a peculiar way and one that, in point of fact, appeared to be getting worse, not better with each new day? Certainly, the wedding wasn't the only reason. Sarah pondered the recent visit from Lady Mornington and Miss Wellesley and the subsequent hastily scheduled fitting with Madame Tizou. It was all so out of the ordinary that she didn't know what to make of it. Then Sarah remembered the earl's suspicion about Mr. Carysfort and Aunt Ophelia being involved in matchmaking. Zeus and Minerva! Could that be why Aunt Ophelia had been acting odd? Although it was impossible to credit, it was the most plausible explanation. Well, if that was the case, Sarah had to inform the earl so they could to put a stop to it. They needed to confer right away.

"You're right, Aunt Ophelia," Sarah said in a tone which she trusted revealed none of her mounting pique. How dare her aunt stoop to anything so low? Sweetly, she concluded, "With the earl's generous offer of assistance I now have the time to go with him after all." She rose to her feet and excused herself to freshen up.

It required no more than three minutes for Sarah to smooth back and secure her hair, locate a bonnet and straighten the bodice of her gown. Glancing in the mirror, she noticed an ink spot on the dress sleeve and grabbed a paisley shawl to cover it. She returned to the drawing room, bade her aunt farewell, and then she and the earl were off to face the Burges Watsons.

"For someone who was most reluctant to set aside your work you certainly were in a hurry to leave," remarked the earl as she led the way toward the Lord Chamberlain's Court, where Mrs. Burges Watson's suite of rooms was located.

Sarah clarified, "It was suddenly of the utmost importance that we talk. I've made the most ghastly discovery."

"Not a corpse or severed head, I trust."

"My lord, I do believe you're a worse tease than

Mr. Carysfort," she remarked. "No, nothing like that."

"What then?"

"You were correct, I'm sad to say." The earl's left brow rose questioningly. She enlightened him. "You were right about Mr. Carysfort and my aunt. They are matchmaking. Although I wasn't in the least bit suspicious when you first mentioned it, Aunt Ophelia has said and done several things over the past days which have been totally out of character. She tried to fob it off to her romantic mood and wedding plans, but compounded by her attitude this afternoon I've no choice but to accept that matchmakers are, indeed, at work in our midst."

A forbidding frown settled upon the earl's features. For Lady Sarah's benefit he managed to hold back a crude oath and muttered instead, "That old dog. I, too, had my suspicions, and was willing to accept your explanations. I didn't really think Max had it in him."

"Nor did I imagine Aunt Ophelia might commit such a traitorous thing," said Sarah with a good measure of righteous indignation.

"We're both betrayed." The earl sounded so much like a third rate thespian in a travelling farce that she couldn't help laughing.

"Thank you for making me laugh. I needed that."

"All is not lost, however, for I do have an idea that may put a stop to Uncle Max and Lady Ophelia." He returned Sarah's smile with equal warmth.

"I should have known I could depend upon a gentleman as experienced as yourself to save us both."

"Do you recall saying that I needed a bodyguard?

Of course, I knew you were jesting, but it made me think of a possible solution. We shall act as foils for one another." His smile transformed to a roguish grin. "That is to say if we create the impression of courting then Uncle Max and Lady Ophelia shall hopefully be satisfied and cease their scheming under the assumption that matters are running their natural course."

This approach was logical and tidy and wholly non-threatening, and so unlike the gentleman that Sarah could not help scrutinizing him with suspicion. "It might work."

"Where's your spirit? Of course, it shall, and in more ways than one. Not only can we deflect my uncle and your aunt, but during the remainder of my stay at the palace I shall enjoy the benefit of your assistance to ward off ambitious females. Will you agree?"

Unable to think of a better solution herself, she gave a reluctant, "Yes."

He was pleased. "How shall I ever repay you?"

"There is a way," Sarah said with a measure of hesitation. It was not in her character to beg favors, especially not from a gentleman of such short acquaintance. Somehow, however, confiding in the earl seemed the right thing to do. She had already shared her views on marriage with him, and as he had endorsed those views she was certain he would understand, if not empathize with her current quandary regarding the social calendar which Aunt Ophelia was determined to inflict upon her.

"Your wish is my command," was his jovial reply.

They had reached the north side of the Base Court, and Sarah paused at the head of the corridor that led to the Lord Chamberlain's Court. His receptive attitude made asking for his assistance easier than she had imagined.

"Might I have your protection, and perhaps, guidance, during the Anglesea ball? Aunt Ophelia and Lady Mornington have taken it upon themselves to accept numerous invitations in my behalf, including some turtle dinner." She gave a shudder. "Aside from the fact that it sounds repulsive, it is one of several forays into Society which I've begun to dread as if it were an advancing plague. I've little talent on a dance floor, know nothing about idle chatter nor the art of flirtation, and I fear I shall become so impatient with all that nonsense that I'll prove a gross discredit to my family's good name."

Radnor stared for a moment at Lady Sarah, thinking how like her it was to worry about her family name when any other young lady would have fretted about her own good standing. "You mustn't concern yourself about any of that, Lady Sarah. Of course, I should be pleased to help in any way I might. You shall not endure turtle dinners or worse without me by your side." Relief registered upon her delicate face causing a responding pang to palpitate within his chest. It was the strangest sensation, but in the next second, it was gone, and feeling like himself once more, he offered her an encouraging grin. "If our deal is done, Lady Sarah, then I suggest we commence our charade immediately. I trust you can do a credible imitation of a young lady pierced by Cupid's dart."

"I shall try, my lord," Sarah cooed, her naturally red lips forming a delightful pucker. She glanced up at the earl from beneath her lashes in such a perfectly coquettish fashion that he almost believed her pretty little head held no thought other than the sentiment that he was the handsomest, most desirable gentleman she had ever set eyes upon.

Egad, the chit was a dandy actress, and Lord Radnor felt himself wanting to satisfy that come hither look by taking her in his arms and kissing her soundly on those luscious lips. Well, he thought, recollecting his earlier vow to steal a kiss from this young lady, there was no better time than the present to see if the sensible Lady Sarah could be ruffled.

His voice dropped to a velvety timbre, and he suggested, "Might we seal our bargain with a kiss?"

Although Sarah knew the earl was assuming his role as ardent suitor, his seductive question nevertheless caused her heart to somersault. This was not the first time he had caused her to react this way, and whether he was genuine or playacting did not matter. She was no more used to his sensual voice and virile presence now than she had been that night in the Clock Court. Her own theatrical facade was fast slipping away, and she swallowed hard as she made a half-turn to face him. Standing an arm's length from his chest, she was overwhelmed by masculine strength, and her heart, scarcely recovered from that violent somersault, began to beat an erratic tattoo.

"A kiss, sir? That's hardly necessary. This is a charade and no one is watching."

"But a little practice could not do any harm." The earl's hands rose to Sarah's shoulders, and he drew her even closer.

"Practice? That's not necessary," she insisted, her breathless voice failing to convey how serious she was.

He merely smiled. The top of her bonnet barely reached his chin, errant strands of soft flaxen hair curled out from beneath the brim to tickle his jawline, and the intoxicating scent of summer roses engulfed his senses. Yes, there was no better time than the present.

"Not necessary?" he teased. "You've vast experience then with kissing, have you?"

"N–no." She was beginning to tremble.

"Ssssh," was all he said, soft and comforting and beguiling as his fingers tightened on her shoulders, and he bent his head toward her upturned face.

Behind them a door opened.

"He's here!" It was Pamela. "Oh, Lord Radnor, how good it is to see you. Mama says to come straight in," she lisped, performed a grandiose curtsy and proceeded to yank the gentleman away from Sarah, whom she acknowledged with only the curtest of nods.

Sarah was not fazed by this snub. She wasn't even aware that she had been slighted. In point of fact, she gave fervent silent thanks for the interruption. The only thing of which she was conscious was the frantic beating of her heart and the unfortunate fact that she'd been about to throw herself upon the earl like some strumpet. Sarah knew an unfamiliar sting of mortification. If she didn't know better, she would have wondered if she and

Aunt Ophelia had both contracted some rare tropical malady. Thank heavens, she had the guise of the charade to blame for her behavior, and the earl would never suspect she hadn't been acting. Stunned by her lack of control, she followed the earl and Pamela into Mrs. Burges Watson's apartment.

Like Lady Ophelia, Mrs. Burges Watson had accommodations in the original palace built by Cardinal Wolsey. Unlike Lady Ophelia's suite, however, Mrs. Burges Watson's was neither as commodious nor as elegant, consisting of merely two rooms for herself, her daughters and a vast quantity of garish furnishings and useless material possessions with which, upon the death of her husband, she had been unable to part company. The earl and Sarah entered the first room that served as a sitting cum dining room to see Mrs. Burges Watson reclining upon a cherry chaise longue covered in flowered needlepoint. The piece was one in a matching suite of two sofas, eight overstuffed arm chairs and six pedestal tables of varying sizes carved with scallop shells and leafage that were crammed into a space designed for less than half as much furniture.

Camilla zigzagged through the maze of furnishings to greet their guests with effusive salutations for the earl, lukewarm for Sarah. Then the sisters, each clinging to one of Radnor's arms, led the gentleman toward a sofa, upon which they deposited their plump forms on either side of him in such a way that they reminded Sarah of a pair of colossal sphinx guarding the plain of El-Gizeh.

Mrs. Burges Watson offered Sarah a no less frosty welcome and directed her toward a chair as far away from the earl as was possible. "Would you mind doing the honors and pouring the tea for us, Lady Sarah?"

It was a contrived question, and Sarah grinned. Mrs. Burges Watson had already set a tea table by her chair. This was, of course, what the woman had intended from the first, and there was no way Sarah could refuse. "I should be happy to do so," she replied, omitting to say that she would appreciate anything which might help to take her mind off the earl and the feelings he aroused in her.

"We heard Madame Tizou visited the palace yesterday," the mother commenced the conversation after demanding a cup of fragrant Couslip with four extra sugar crystals.

Sarah gave a nod as she poured boiling water through a sadly tarnished silver tea strainer that looked as if it had seen better days. "Yes, she came at Lady Mornington's request."

"Madame Tizou didn't make *that* outfit, did she?" Camilla peered down the length of her nose at Sarah's bishop's blue dress and paisley shawl. The color was most out-of-fashion, and only an ape leader would own a paisley shawl.

"No, my ball gown will be my first outfit from madame."

"*You're* to have a Tizou!" Pamela exclaimed.

"But I thought you said she went to see the countess," lisped Camilla.

"She did, but Aunt Ophelia felt I needed a new gown for the Season and Lady Mornington kindly included me in the fitting session."

The three women failed to disguise their dismay. This was Mrs. Burges Watson's worst nightmare: Lady Sarah dressed in one of Madame Tizou's gowns and on the Town for the Season.

"*Only* your first?" needled the zealous mama. "Madame always makes the girl's dresses, y'know. What do you think of their gowns, Lord Radnor?"

"Aren't they grand?" Camilla fluttered her eyelashes at the earl while Pamela bounced upon the needlepoint cushion several times to get him to look away from her sister.

Despite these vulgar shenanigans, there was no expression upon the earl's face when he spoke. "In matters of fashion I must defer to female judgment. Lady Sarah, please tell us what you think."

What Sarah thought was that the discerning and talented French modiste had likely designed those outfits under extreme duress. The bodices were shockingly low and the waists were pinched in lending a ghastly out-of-proportion appearance to the weighty wearers. There was an excess of gee gaws adorning the sleeves and about the hemlines that had been dyed the most iridescent shades of green and pink upon which Sarah had ever set her eyes.

"The colors are very bright." She chose her words with great care. Kindness mingled with a hint of sympathy in her voice. It wasn't that Sarah considered herself better than the Burges Watson twins, rather she knew the futility of their outlandish behavior. The poor girls and their mama didn't realize that there was nothing that could ever make the earl think highly of them, or any female, for that matter.

"Mama says vivid colors distinguish flowers from weeds," Pamela lisped in a superior tone. "You should wear brighter colors, Lady Sarah."

"Mama says *you're* old enough, y'know."

At this bold affrontery, the earl's bland facade vanished to be replaced by open outrage. How dare these ill-bred creatures insult Lady Sarah? In a razor sharp tongue, he retorted, "It's not Lady Sarah's age, but her beauty that would entitle her to brilliant colors. Although I've always held with the credo that one must not gild a lily, and as Lady Sarah is as magnificent as a rare lily I would not want to see that splendor obscured."

Sarah's eyes flew open wide and twin dots of hot color flared upon her cheeks. Then she remembered their charade and demurely lowered her eyelashes to stare at the tea tray.

Although the Burges Watson twins spared no tricks in their efforts to outshine Lady Sarah, her natural dignity and feminine poise could not be undermined. In point of fact, the harder they tried, the better she appeared to Radnor. She was, he thought, the most radiant female he had seen in an age, particularly when he was able to make her blush like a schoolgirl.

At length, she looked up from her regard of the tea tray. "Lord Radnor, I see Mrs. Burges Watson has several varieties of tea. What is your pleasure, sir?"

He was staring at her luscious red lips and recalling the smell of summer roses and those moments in the corridor when she had stood so close. "Is there any gunpowder?" he asked in a low silky voice.

She shivered and tried to look away, but his smoldering gaze pulled hers like a magnet. "Yes," she replied, her own voice sounding to her ears as if it were coming from far off. Her heart was pounding again, drowning out the very sound of her voice. Horrified by such an uncontrollable reaction, she glanced at the other occupants of the room. Could they hear the pounding of her heart? There was a tiny tremble in her hand when she poured out water for the earl's tea.

What folly had she committed to agree that they feign courtship when being in his company produced this unnatural effect upon her? She was supposed to have been on guard for the unusual, but in her overreaction to the discovery of Aunt Ophelia's perfidy she had failed. Such impulsive behavior made her an ideal candidate for Bedlam. Well, she couldn't back out of their charade, but what was she to do? Quickly, she turned the question over in her mind. The best course was to be logical, honest and direct with herself and the earl. She would just have to tell him to moderate the charade. She would have to inform him that no matter how convincing it might be he was *never* again to touch her in any way.

9

"THAT SCANT EXCUSE for a mother was positively the most odious, insufferable parvenu I've ever had the misfortune to encounter." The earl was pacing back and forth across the carpet in Boodle's coffee room at a furious rate. He and Mr. Carysfort had made the twelve-mile journey into London to welcome the dowager countess to the family town house overlooking Park Lane. The lady was about to have the last of her two worldly wishes realized—her son, Maximillian, was at last to be married, and she could hope that her grandson, Beverly, would soon follow suit. This was cause for celebration, and upon hearing the news of her youngest son's betrothal, the elderly lady had decided to quit Temple Radnor and enjoy the Season in London. The dowager maintained country hours and following an excruciatingly early breakfast, the gentlemen had stopped in at their club.

The earl continued to cut a path back and forth across the floor. "And the daughters. Pamela and Camilla. Mushrooms, I tell you, and as puffed up as they get."

"I could have told you that," rejoined Mr. Carysfort from behind the latest issue of the *Morning Chronicle*. Aside from the club's superlative chef, the greatest pleasure Mr. Carysfort derived from his membership at Boodle's was ready access to pressed copies of all the daily papers.

Radnor cast his relative a peevish *Well, why didn't you tell me?* glance, and without missing a step he ranted on, "Why old Maryborough didn't pay off that miserable parvenu instead of letting her marry his son, no matter how worthless he may have been, I'll never comprehend."

"They are rather ragmannered. As you're being right now," Mr. Carysfort pointed out. "Do sit down, Beverly, or you'll have every tongue in Mayfair wagging before noon."

A quick glance about the coffee room satisfied the earl that the only other members present were Beauchamp and de Monfort, both so doddering they'd not notice the advance of Bonaparte's *Moyenne Garde* should they march past the bow window. Radnor paid no heed to Mr. Carysfort's admonition and continued his tirade. "Ragmannered is putting it mildly. You should have seen how those Burges Watson creatures treated Lady Sarah. I've seen some appalling behavior in my time, but this was beyond the pale. Lady Sarah isn't often abused like that, is she?"

"Not as a general rule, but you must own she's an unusual female and does elicit some adverse attention."

"Unusual she may be, but she's miles above those insipid upstarts." His voice rose in outrage. "They're not fit to polish her boots."

Mr. Carysfort lowered his paper to scrutinize the earl. He'd never seen his nephew in such a pother over any female, except perhaps the time that lovely Irish cyprian had left him for a Philadelphia banker. This rather passionate display was far more than he and Lady Ophelia had dared to hope might develop in such a short time, and Mr. Carysfort knew the earl had to be skillfully cultivated. "Lady Sarah has a champion in you, I see," was his restrained observation.

The earl's pacing came to an abrupt halt. "Yes, I suppose you're right," he said with the startling realization that he wasn't acting a part for the charade. This anger and this concern for Lady Sarah were real. Stunned by this, he subsided into the nearest claw-footed armchair with a thump.

"You must care about her a great deal," said Mr. Carysfort in such a way that his statement was more query than fact.

"Of course I care about her," he retorted. The earl did not like anyone being able to read his feelings as if they were an open book, particularly when those feelings involved a woman. Instinctively, he tried to downplay the significance of his concern. "Why shouldn't I be concerned? After all, Lady Sarah is your fiance's niece and—"

"She has the most astonishingly glorious hair." Mr. Carysfort flashed the earl a wry and knowing smile.

"Yes, that too," he said, thankful for his uncle's lighter mood. In the next moment, he remembered the charade and took refuge behind the facade it provided. He embellished, "Glorious hair and sparkling eyes and the most kissable lips I've ever beheld."

"Kissable lips! Precisely what are your intentions toward Lady Sarah?" demanded Mr. Carysfort. The purpose of throwing the pair together without a chaperone was a betrothal, not a seduction. Had matters gone awry? He'd admitted to a stolen kiss upon their first encounter. Had he taken more than that? "Lady Ophelia won't countenance your playing fast and loose with the girl, y'know. And neither will I."

"My intentions? Aren't you rushing things just a bit, Max? Although I must admit such considerations would not be out of the realm of possibility," he said for the benefit of the charade. "Lady Sarah is a welcome change from the normal crop of females, and I enjoy her company, but as for *her* feelings about me and her expectations, I can't say. You must give us time to get to know one another better before I might discuss the subject of intentions." Time enough, he thought, for the season to pass, for you to marry Lady Ophelia and depart on your wedding trip, and for Lady Sarah and myself to abandon the charade and go about our own lives.

Had Mr. Carysfort known what the earl was thinking he would not have been pleased, but the earl's words were precisely what Mr. Carysfort wanted to hear, and he nearly dropped the *Morning Chronicle* in his excitement at this promising statement from his nephew. "Yes, of course. Time. Time's always a factor. Didn't mean to be overbearing. Just wanted to make sure everything was on the up and up."

A grin settled upon Radnor's countenance. "Oh, indeed, it is. Everything's on the up and up." His grin deepened, an idea taking shape in his mind. Silently, the earl made a personal pledge to pursue intentions of the most honorable degree. He would, indeed, play the role of Lady Sarah's champion, her knight. At the Anglesea ball he would shield her from snide glances or sharp remarks, he would see that her dance card was filled, that she was introduced to all the right people and that she was surrounded by admiring gentlemen. In short, he would do everything within his power to guarantee she enjoy herself to the fullest. Verily, he resolved to make certain Lady Sarah Clement-Brooke was declared the belle of the season.

April turned to May, and the days until the Anglesea ball flew by in a flurry of activity. Sarah sat several late afternoon vigils with the earl in the Old Court House. Mr. Carysfort organized an outing on the Thames. The Ladies Sarah and Ophelia made their regular visit to the churchyard in Teddington. And Madame Tizou made two additional visits to the palace for fittings with Sarah and Miss Wellesley, who despite the protestations of her parents, got the magenta velvet gown she had always desired. "With war on the horizon there's no telling who might be in mourning before the Season's over," the Countess of Mornington had advocated in behalf of her great-granddaughter. "Let the child enjoy herself while she can."

As for Sarah her gown was a confection of amethyst silk which, as Miss Wellesley had predicted, was the perfect color to highlight the unique violet shade of her eyes and the soft texture of her flaxen hair. Madame had withheld not an ounce of her talent in the design of Sarah's gown. To have so lovely a young lady wear one of her creations was an opportunity to promote her talents. The shrewd Frenchwoman knew only too well that owing to the nation of her birth her recently acquired reputation was in serious jeopardy, and she was banking on the prospect that when the ladies of the upper ten thousand saw Lady Sarah's amethyst silk gown they would all demand a Tizou no matter what the outcome of the situation on the Continent.

After much experimentation it was the seed pearls richly embroidered against the delicate Florence satin that provided the appropriate lushness Lady Sarah deserved, while a broad sash, plaited bodice and full skirt accentuated her perfect figure. The help of four seamstresses had been required to stitch thousands of seed pearls in bouquets about the deep flounce and full shoulders. After many hours of work it was done, and when Sarah had tried on the finished gown Madame Tizou had gasped in delight—although the dress was not the current style, it would set style—and Lady Ophelia had smiled at the transformation of her niece from Bluestocking to Incomparable. Like Sarah, the gown was unique. It highlighted her niece's beauty which had been hidden far too long.

"*Merveilleux!*" Madame had declared secure in the belief that her career was assured. "You must allow me to outfit you for the Season, *mademoi-*

selle. It would be my greatest honor." And so it was agreed by Lady Ophelia that Madame Tizou would design a complete new wardrobe for Sarah, who was astounded at the number of walking outfits and riding habits, afternoon dresses, dancing frocks and ball gowns that were soon to be in her possession.

It was half past three on the afternoon of the ball, Lady Mornington's entourage of traveling coaches was scheduled to depart for Anglesea House on Hanover Square at five o'clock, and with less than two hours to spare Sarah sat at her dressing table hostage to her aunt and her aunt's abigail, Gussie. Her hair was in curl papers to render it manageable, if not stylish, and gobs of Roman balsam were slathered upon her face, down her neck and across her shoulders. This was the work of Aunt Ophelia and Gussie, and feeling utterly helpless, Sarah put her chin on her hands, stared at her reflection and wrinkled her brow at the ghastly sight.

"You're not going to subject me to a chin strap, are you?"

Lady Ophelia made a wounded moue. "Don't tell me you don't appreciate all of this."

"We'll never be ready." Sarah's nerves had been on edge since daybreak. It was difficult enough to brace herself to attend the ball without appearing a total wreck, but as the time neared she found herself becoming more and more anxious about the earl and their charade. The gentleman had agreed to pose as her suitor, but who would believe such a thing? Who would ever believe that the unremarkable Lady Sarah Clement-Brooke could attract the notice of the Earl of Radnor? Just as she worried that she might bring shame upon her family name, she harbored misgivings that she might not be able to carry off the charade, and in failing to do so would exacerbate rather than diminish the earl's problems. She did not worry for herself, but was concerned that she would disappoint the earl.

"Oh, do stop fretting. My goodness, Sarah, I never thought *you'd* pitch into such a state over a mere social engagement. You shall be ready in time and all this fuss shall have been well worth it. I promise," said Lady Ophelia as she directed Gussie to wipe off the Roman balsam.

The abigail, long frustrated that her mistress did not usually participate in the Season's festivities, was thrilled that Lady Ophelia had finally decided to do otherwise, and the lady's maid had been more than happy to again practice her expert skills as a dresser and stylist. It was Gussie who had decided upon the perfect coiffure for Sarah, an artful combination of a loose knot at the crown à la Greque from which ringlets à la Sevigne entwined with silk roses and satin ribbons cascaded over one shoulder. Having wiped off the Roman balsam, the abigail turned her attention to the arrangement of Lady Sarah's hair.

Thirty-five minutes later it was time to slip on Madame Tizou's gown, and Sarah knew a renewed stab of apprehension. Soon she would be in the carriage and on her way to Town and whatever the evening held there could be no avoiding it.

Sarah stood and stepped into the circle of petticoats and satin. The gown was lifted and she slipped her arms into the sleeves. None too patiently, she waited while Gussie fastened the row of tiny mother-of-pearl buttons that ran up her back.

"Oh, my lady, 'tis a vision you are," enthused Gussie as she admired her handiwork, and Lady Ophelia agreed that Sarah was bound to cause a stir at the ball.

The initial impression Sarah gave was ethereal. The seed pearls sparkled like distant stars against the amethyst satin, and she looked like an angel walking among the pale mauve clouds of a magnificent sunset. Upon a first glimpse, she appeared as untouchable as the stars in the heavens. The next impression, however, was of unparalleled feminine allure, for every aspect of the gown to the finest detail complimented Lady Sarah's delicate face and shapely figure, and any man gazing at Lady Sarah would entertain thoughts far from the untouchable variety.

"You must see for yourself, my dear. Come." Lady Ophelia bestowed an encouraging smile upon Sarah as she led her to the pier glass in the corner of the room.

Seeing herself, Sarah was rendered speechless. That sophisticated creature staring back at her bore no similarity to Sarah's image of herself, and while she didn't imagine gentlemen harboring lusty desires for her, she did recognize that a miracle had been accomplished. She did, indeed, present a breathtaking vision. A new found self-confidence came to Sarah. The earl would not be disappointed when he saw her; no one would doubt that she had attracted the notice of the Earl of Radnor.

Making a little half-turn to gaze upon her reflection from the side, Sarah knew an uncharacteristic skirl of feminine vanity. It was amazing, she mused, how nothing more than a few yards of fabric could change one's outlook. Of a sudden, Sarah was quite looking forward to the Anglesea ball, and in particular, to playing her role of besotted sweetheart with the Earl of Radnor. In point of fact, she altogether forgot how important it was to keep a safe distance between herself and the earl.

10

DURING THE SEASON even the most modest *at home* was responsible for terrible congestion in the narrow streets of Mayfair, and it was no surprise that the popular Anglesea ball created a veritable bottleneck as a line of elegant town coaches moved at a snail's pace up Carlos Place, past Grosvenor Square and into Brook Street. Thirty or forty minutes could quite easily be required to travel less than one-sixth of a mile in the West End, and it would have been far faster and simpler to get out and walk, but no one dreamed of indulging in such a plebeian faux pas.

Thus it was that Sarah and the earl, and Lady Ophelia and Mr. Carysfort remained in the hired travelling carriage behind a vehicle carrying Miss Wellesley, her parents, and the Countess of Mornington, who was making one of her rare appearances in Society. Their destination on Hanover Square was a mansion with a fine Palladian front and an elegant iron arch over the entrance from which lanterns were suspended. On either side of the front steps of Anglesea House stood link boys in glossy silk hats and scarlet waistcoats; they were carrying square lanterns, and when the carriage in which Sarah was riding came to a stop they hurried forward to open the door and light the way.

Inside the mansion, gentlemen in formal black evening wear and jewel-laden ladies were packed cheek-to-jowl. Liveried servants stood sentry at the foot of a sweeping marble staircase that was festooned with ivy and sweet-scented gardenias, and enormous bouquets of dark purple gladioli. Holland tulips in crimson, and ivory sweetbriar roses graced carved Doric pedestals throughout the first floor vestibule.

The Ladies Ophelia and Sarah, Miss Wellesley and the Countess of Mornington made a brief stop in the ladies' cloakroom to deposit their wraps after which they rejoined the gentlemen and proceeded to the second floor where Lord and Lady Anglesea were receiving their guests. Requisite pleasantries were exchanged, the countess retired to the balcony where the other dowagers were seated, and the rest of the party from Hampton Court made its way into the ballroom, where Miss Wellesley and her parents were joined by her fiancé and his parents.

While the return to Town of the Earl of Radnor was duly noted, it was the exquisite flaxen-haired beauty upon his arm that caused a wave of gossip to wend its way through Anglesea House. It began upon the ladies' departure from the cloakroom, where the assembled ingenues and their mamas speculated upon the origins of Lady Sarah's shimmering pearl-embroidered gown, then it spread to the ballroom.

" 'Pon my soul," drawled a dandy, whose jacket with a pinched-in waist gave him the appearance of a garden aphid. "Believe I've just seen a goddess."

"Radnor always did have all the luck," one of his companions remarked. The gentlemen were hovering in an alcove beneath the ballroom balcony, a vantage point which afforded them a perfect view of all the evening's comings and goings.

A third member of the party raised an ornate quizzing glass to study the couple. "And do we think we're smelling of April and May?"

"With a heavenly beauty like that? I should think so," said the Aphid.

"Does anyone know who she is?" The gentleman with the quizzing glass continued to peer at Sarah with the sort of scrutiny a biologist dedicates to a rare specimen.

"Believe it's Lady Sarah."

"Clement-Brooke?"

"Thought she was at her last prayer and living with a maiden aunt."

"Your source is obviously unreliable," drawled the Aphid, his gaze never wavering from the lovely lady.

On the balcony above the gentlemen, the dowager Countess of Glenbervie, who was several years past ninety and stone deaf, spoke in an over-loud voice to her mousy companion, a penniless distaff relative from Northumberland. "There's that rogue Radnor. Always did say the gentleman had a nice pair of legs. Swear I can see the muscles from here.

Who's the chit on his arm? Lucky gel." The elderly lady's high-pitched voice carried down the row of the dowagers, fourteen turbaned heads turned to stare at Lady Glenbervie, and the young woman from Northumberland cringed.

"It's Chelsea's granddaughter," supplied the Countess of Mornington.

"Chelsea? Haven't seen him in ages. Where's the darling man?"

"Thought he was dead."

"He is. It's his granddaughter," clarified Lady Mornington. "Lady Sarah Clement-Brooke."

"They're betrothed, you say? Did you hear, Lady Agatha?" Lady Glenbervie addressed a sparrow-like octogenarian. "That handsome devil Radnor's to marry at last!"

"Who?" Lady Agatha could not see beyond the lace cuff of her bombazine gown, and she turned a blind squint over the balcony railing.

"That gorgeous creature on his arm."

"Caught Radnor, did she?" Lady Agatha chirped. "Must be a remarkable gel. When's the wedding?"

For a second, the Countess of Mornington considered putting a stop to this rampant tale. In the next instant, she thought better of it. A tidbit of gossip featuring Lady Sarah and the earl could do no harm. In fact, it might even help to make the pair realize how perfectly matched they were. Yes, a little gossip was just what was needed she decided as she watched the earl go through the motions of introducing Lady Sarah to several of his acquaintances.

"Allow me to present Lady Sarah Clement-Brooke," said Radnor with such effusive honor that not even the most jaded roué might have suspected his attentiveness toward the lady was less than genuine. Tilting his head sideways, his clear blue eyes sought her violet ones, and he offered an encouraging smile as he rattled off the names of the surrounding ladies and gentlemen. He began with the Earl and Countess of Conyngham, whose marriage of convenience was one in which both husband and wife enjoyed numerous affaires. Next, he introduced Lady Diana Ryder, and her cousin, the Marquess of Egremont, one of the Ton's most vicious tattlemongers. Standing beside the marquess was Sir Benjamin Westmacott, whose misfortunes at the faro table had reduced him to dealing with Israelitish gullgropers until he might marry an heiress. Completing the circle was the Duke of Carlisle with his sister, Lady Charlotte Harrowby, a lady known to frequently engage in the most public and disgraceful competition for the Earl of Radnor's attentions. The gentlemen signed Lady Sarah's dance card, and the ladies fluttered about Radnor like a flock of canaries, hanging upon his every word as if he possessed the wisdom of Solomon.

Sir Benjamin was the first to speak to Sarah. "We're neighbors I believe, Lady Sarah. Aren't you at No. 12 South Audley?"

"Number twelve is my brother's home, but he's in Palestine, and the house has been let for several years."

The gentleman was visibly disappointed in this intelligence. "But don't you plan to take up residence in Town?" Sir Benjamin inquired in the hopes of gleaning a better picture of Lady Sarah's financial circumstances.

"That does not seem necessary," Sarah said in her usual forthright manner. "My aunt and I are guests of the Earl of Radnor and his grandmother."

"For the whole of the Season?" This came from the Earl of Conyngham. He studied Sarah with a bold eye that hinted of seduction.

Radnor frowned, and telling himself it was for the sake of the charade, he assumed a proprietary tone. "Gentlemen, I'm afraid I have the most unfortunate news. Lady Sarah is only in Town for a brief stay."

Sarah nearly blushed at Radnor's choice of words, and offering a charming smile to the assembled gentlemen, she expanded, "We came for the express purpose of attending this ball, and our visit shall also include the opera tomorrow evening. My aunt wishes to see Amalia Rosetti perform Cherubino in *Le Nozze di Figaro* at the Royal Italian Opera House."

"I hear Rosetti has been in fine form," remarked Conyngham putting blatant emphasis on *fine form* as his gaze raked over Lady Sarah.

The earl's frown deepened to a definite scowl. Too well did he recall his first encounter with Lady Sarah and how the sight of her magnificent curls and pert red lips had turned his mind in a wholly licentious direction. No doubt Conyngham was entertaining similar thoughts. Perhaps, the earl reconsidered, striving to make Lady Sarah a belle was not such a commendable goal after all.

"How did you manage to come by opera tickets?" inquired Sir Benjamin. Someone who seldom visited Town would hardly be able to obtain seats for such a heralded performance.

"My aunt has always maintained a box, and although she doesn't use it as often as she might wish, it is a convenience she has vowed never to relinquish."

Sir Benjamin's spirits rose. An opera box was a sizable expense, often in the neighborhood of two thousand pounds. Lady Sarah's aunt was obviously a woman of independent means, a fact which boded well for Sir Benjamin, who had only that morning suffered the most unpleasant visit from the duns. At best, an aunt with plump pockets could mean a niece of means; at the least, it meant a generous marriage settlement. This introduction to Lady Sarah was providential, and it would be wise to cultivate the lady's acquaintance. He performed a quick mental computation to determine whether or not he could afford to hire a carriage, then inquired, "Might I have the honor of calling upon you at Lord Radnor's for a carriage ride, Lady Sarah? You must not leave the metropolis without having enjoyed a circuit of the park."

"That is a kind offer, sir, but I fear there shall be no time for such a pleasure. Tomorrow afternoon, I accompany my friend the Countess of Mornington to Lady Russburough's, and my aunt and I shall be returning home the morning after the opera."

"And where is home?" injected Lady Charlotte, who having been last Season's reigning Incomparable did not like the way the assembled gentlemen were ogling this newcomer. Lady Sarah was an unknown, and how she had managed to attract such attention without so much as a single flirtatious glance or flutter of her fan was a mystery. It was a most annoying situation, particularly since

Lady Sarah had managed to succeed where she had failed. Apparently, Lady Sarah had accomplished the impossible; she had conquered Lord Radnor's haughty and heretofore impenetrable demeanor.

"Home is at Hampton Court."

"You live in grace and favor?" This was said with obvious condescension, for the general opinion was that only the indigent or incontinent were forced to resort to such a housekeeping arrangement.

"Yes, with my aunt, Lady Ophelia. Perhaps you would like to visit some day, Lady Charlotte, and you, too, Sir Benjamin, and Lord and Lady Conyngham?" Sarah's offer was both gracious and ingenuous. This evening was not the ordeal she had feared it might be, and Sarah found herself as composed as if she were chatting with neighbors in Aunt Ophelia's drawing room. "I'm always more than happy to show off the palace. It has a marvelous history, you know, and the gardens are quite without compare."

"A visit? Perhaps," came Lady Charlotte's disdainful reply which seemed to imply that the only thing more tedious than the prospect of a jaunt to Hampton Court was conversation with Lady Sarah.

Radnor observed Lady Charlotte and ill-concealed anger crossed his handsome face. It was bad enough that ladies of supposed good birth comported themselves like strumpets when it came to snaring a husband, but to abuse another lady was beyond the pale. Lady Charlotte was an uncharitable snob, and Radnor opined that her conduct had managed to eclipse even that of the Burges Watson twins. Whoever had conceived that polite society was an apt reference to London's upper ten thousand was sadly misguided. It was more like a snake pit, and Radnor was beginning to regret that Lady Sarah should have to be exposed to it.

"Hampton Court is quite fashionable these days, dear sister," remarked the Duke of Carlisle, who knew that if Lady Charlotte had not already done so, she was perilously close to repulsing a highly eligible parti.

"Fashionable?" someone remarked with a doubtful sneer.

"Indeed." Carlisle forced a smile. "I hear Radnor is in residence these days."

A murmur of surprise rippled about the circle.

"You don't say."

"How quaint."

"In that case, I should like to reconsider your invitation, Lady Sarah, for I should never like to be thought unfashionable," said Lady Charlotte without a hint a shame.

At this point, Radnor's disgust with Lady Charlotte changed to vexation with Lady Sarah. She was supposed to keep females such as Lady Charlotte at bay, not invite them to invade his retreat at Hampton Court. He did not temper his aggravation when he spoke.

"Lady Sarah is extremely gracious, but we are a bit busy for visitors, aren't we, Lady Sarah? Perhaps you might wait and visit in September, Lady Charlotte," he suggested knowing full well that Carlisle and Lady Charlotte would by that time have returned to the country for the autumn grouse shoot.

"Busy? The pair of you?" the Marquess of Egremont dangled for a prime bit of tattle. Scrutinizing

Radnor and Lady Sarah he could not help suspecting there was something between them, and he hoped his suspicions were about to be confirmed. Gossip about Radnor was always elevating, and if Egremont were to have the inside track on the earl's newest interest, it could mean netting some healthy profits from the betting books at White's.

"Yes, *we're* busy." The earl's jaw muscles tightened. He could read Egremont like an open book, and he experienced a compelling urge to call him out for even daring to consider such scandalous thoughts about Lady Sarah. This was no mere snake pit to which he had introduced Sarah, but a nest of poisonous vipers. All the more reason to persist in their charade. Although nothing might prevent Egremont from gossiping, Radnor's attentions would hopefully protect Sarah from the likes of Sir Benjamin and Lord Conyngham. He cast a suitably besotted smile upon Sarah. "I'm assisting Lady Sarah with her work."

"And what work is that?" There was a malicious glimmer in Egremont's eyes.

"Ghost hunting," Sarah supplied with her usual measure of effusiveness. "To be specific, a spirit that has been haunting Sir Christopher Wren's house in the palace garden."

The ladies gasped, reticules clicked open, and the sharp scent of recuperative salts pierced the air. The Countess of Conyngham actually took two steps backward.

"I did not know you had an interest in the supernatural, my lord," simpered Lady Charlotte.

"Neither did I until Lady Sarah explained her work. It's most fascinating, and her theories are

more than plausible." In the hopes of boring Lady
Charlotte to tears, he added, "Did you know there
may be a plane of existence between life and death,
and that spirits are merely souls shackled by their
grief to a particular spot on this earth?"

Radnor's strategy failed. There was little anyone
might do to fend off Lady Charlotte. She was determined to let nothing stand in her way and would
likely have crossed the Channel to confront the
entire French army, if doing so meant gaining the
gentleman's favor. She fluttered her eyelashes over
the edge of her japaned fan. "I saw a ghost once at
my grandfather's estate. In the wedding chamber,
to be precise."

"Mayhap his lordship could perform an exor-
cism," sniped Egremont.

The orchestra struck up the opening chords of a
minuet, putting a halt to the deteriorating conversation. Sir Benjamin claimed Lady Sarah, and the
earl, who never danced unless the lady was happily
married or an elderly relative, lounged against an
ornamental pilaster and observed the couples forming sets. Usually at about this time, he retreated to
the card room, but because of Lady Sarah he didn't
do so this evening. His presence would lend credence to their charade, but more important, none
of those gentlemen were to be trusted, and it was
his duty as Lady Sarah's self-appointed champion
to keep a watchful eye on her. While it appeared
he was not needed to guarantee her social success,
she did require his protection.

Following the minuet, Lady Sarah was partnered
with the Duke of Carlisle for a gavotte, the Marquess
of Egremont for an ecossaise, and then Mr. Carysfort

appeared to lead her through the steps of a Scottish reel. Despite the lady's unfavorable opinion of her abilities on the dance floor, Lady Sarah was a more than adequate dancer, and Radnor rather enjoyed watching her execute the various patterns of curtseys and turns and entrechats. Verily, the earl actually found himself wishing Lady Sarah's dance card was not full, for he would gladly have broken his self-imposed restrictions for dancing, if it meant partnering such a graceful lady. Thank goodness he had had the foresight to pencil his name in for dinner. There was one more dance before the break, and then he might warn her about Egremont's malicious tongue, the Earl of Conyngham's adulterous eye, and Sir Benjamin's addiction to the green baize.

The triple time notes of a mazurka resounded through the ballroom, and there was an enchanting smile upon Lady Sarah's pretty face as her next partner approached for the lively Polish folk dance. It was the Earl of Conyngham, noted Radnor with visible outrage. How dare the man claim Lady Sarah for more than one dance! Clearly, he possessed not a shred of decency to behave in a way that was guaranteed to put Lady Sarah's name upon every tongue in Christendom. If Radnor didn't do something, the wags were going to make a nine day wonder of Lady Sarah. With no care save protecting her from an adverse connection with Conyngham, the earl pushed away from the pilaster and in four purposeful strides crossed the dance floor to stand before Lady Sarah and Conyngham. His grin was dangerous, and his blue eyes had darkened considerably.

Sarah was puzzled. "My lord?"

Conyngham, however, was no fool. He knew why Radnor was looming before them and sporting an ominous expression. He stammered, "I believe my wife is motioning to me. Would you excuse me, Lady Sarah? I trust Lord Radnor will step in for me." He gave a curt bow and disappeared into the crowd.

In a quick movement, Radnor slipped an arm about Sarah's waist and began to guide her off the dance floor.

What was going on? Looking for an explanation, Sarah gazed up at the earl, but instead of finding reassurance she was further confused as the most unsettling sensation assailed her limbs. Of a sudden, she was decidedly weak-kneed, and there was no doubt in her mind as to the cause. *He* was much too close. Until this moment, she had managed to forget about telling Radnor that he must not touch her in any way, and now when the opportunity for private speech presented itself her message was of paramount and immediate importance. To mask her confusion, she pinned a sweet smile upon her face, but her words were not so sweet. She whispered in a sharp tone, "You must not hold me so close, my lord."

Staring straight ahead, the earl pulled her even closer to his side. "It is rather warm in here," he said in a low smooth voice that revealed none of his emotions as he led her through a pair of open doors and on to the balcony.

"I believe you're jealous, my lord," said Sarah in as steady a voice as possible. Her heart was pounding at a furious rate, and while she wasn't sure of the veracity of her statement it was the first thing that popped out of her mouth.

"Of course, I'm jealous," he retorted, some of his anger surfacing to be reflected in his tone of voice. "Supposed to be courting you, ain't I? And you're out there cavorting like this was your last night before you faced the gallows. Didn't Lady Ophelia ever tell you not to dance with the same gentleman more than once in an evening? People will talk, and it won't be nice."

"What in heaven's name could anyone find to say? After all Lord Conyngham is a married man."

Radnor stared hard at Sarah. "Are you truly so naive?"

"I suppose so, for I've no idea what you're hinting at." She returned his direct gaze. Her heartbeat slowed, and she tilted her delicate chin upward in a gesture that was both defiant and provocative. "I was merely enjoying myself, my lord. Having never been the object of so much attention, I find it's rather nice, and if there's some nefarious plot afoot, you must enlighten me."

"Nice!" His voice rose in disbelief. "They're all scheming how they might best use you for their personal benefit. Besides which it isn't right for a lady whom I've been courting to keep company with the likes of Conyngham. He may be married, but the man's a notorious adulterer."

Her bright violet eyes snapped with her own anger. "You're acting like I've done something wrong, but I haven't, y'know. None of this is my doing. If anyone's at fault, it's you, my lord, for having introduced them to me. Besides which no one's watching us now so you needn't continue with the charade. Please let go of me."

He didn't know whether to shake her or to laugh. "You're being impertinent, Lady Sarah."

She flashed a gamine smile. "I believe you once called me an ill-bred serving wench."

"Don't change the subject. We must be vigilant and maintain the charade at all times. We can never know when someone might be peering from behind the draperies."

"Peering from behind draperies," she repeated on a giggle. "If they are, I'm certain a squabble is hardly the sort of sight they were hoping to witness."

"How true." He grinned. There was a wicked glimmer in his eyes. "Shall we remedy that?"

Sarah opened her mouth to tell him it depended upon what that remedy might be, but speech eluded her as he lifted her hand to his mouth. She watched in fascination. With exquisite deliberateness, the earl placed a lingering kiss upon her palm, and even through the kid fabric of her evening glove she felt the warmth of that kiss. The kiss ended. He raised his head, their eyes met, and she gazed at him. His lips were moving, he was saying something to her, but she heard not a word as she closed her fingers about the palm that burned from the imprint of his lips.

"You must not touch me like that, my lord," she entreated in a husky whisper.

"And why is that, my lady?" His voice was low and soft, and he couldn't resist running a finger up her arm and stopping just below the shoulder of her gown to draw a small taunting circle at that spot no more than a fraction of an inch from her bare skin. "Why shouldn't I touch you?" His other arm that remained wrapped about her waist hugged her closer.

Sarah shivered. It seemed as if his very words reached out to caress her, and she swallowed hard before she might reply. "While we may wish to give the impression of courting, we certainly don't wish to do anything that shall appear compromising and thereby force you to do the right. I thought our primary purpose was to avoid matrimony, not to force the issue."

Radnor knew Lady Sarah was correct. As usual she was making perfect sense. In point of fact, it was too logical, and the earl couldn't help believing there was some other reason why the lady didn't want him so close. Could it be, he wondered, that his proximity did, indeed, ruffle Lady Sarah? Could it be that beneath that composed exterior there was a vulnerable woman with passionate sensibilities? He remembered how she had trembled when he'd kissed her that night in the Clock Court. Could it be he was the man destined to breathe life into that dormant sensual creature? It was a surprising and not altogether unpleasant prospect, and he couldn't douse the pulse of desire he experienced at the thought that his touch affected her.

He gazed down at Sarah. A light breeze rippled through the Anglesea garden, in the trees above them the leaves rustled like paper coins, and Lady Sarah's soft flaxen curls danced a delicate pattern about her face. The clouds drifted to the edges of the ebony sky, and moonlight streamed down to wash her upturned face in its silver light. Her cherry lips were parted as if waiting for his touch, and those wide violet eyes seemed to have lost their innocence as she returned his smoldering gaze. The sweet jasmine fragrance of early spring roses tantalized his senses, and he recalled the small inarticulate sound that had escaped Lady Sarah when he had kissed her in the Clock Court.

Desire tightened within him, and he feared that if he didn't kiss her he might burst from wanting. He lifted his hand from her shoulder to cup her chin, but in the next instant, he stopped, let go of her altogether and took a step backward.

What was the matter with him? Had he lost his senses? What if he had allowed himself to taste those lips as fully and intimately as he wished? What if someone were watching? He knew the answer. One compromising bit of gossip and they'd be walking down the aisle at St. George's.

He gave an awkward cough, and unable to meet her eyes, he said, "We should join Lady Ophelia and my uncle. They're waiting for us in the dining room."

Sarah breathed a sigh of relief. "Of course. We must not keep them waiting." That wobbly sensation in her legs began to abate, and feeling more like her usual self, she said in a lighter tenor, "By the by, my lord, I take it you don't wish me to ride in the park with Sir Benjamin should the opportunity present itself."

Radnor mumbled his reply and changed the subject. While Lady Sarah appeared recovered from those moments on the terrace, Radnor was not, and he was deep in thought as they strolled to the dining room.

This was a dangerous game he was playing. His emotions had run a gauntlet this night, and he knew that if he were a less experienced gentleman, his heart *and his future* might be in grave danger. It was time, he decided, to pay a visit to his ballet dancer.

11

"GONE OFF TO visit a ballet dancer!" Lady Ophelia exclaimed with visible dismay as she sprang from a velvet covered chair. She and Mr. Carysfort were dressed for the opera, and they were waiting for Sarah in the Adam's Room of the earl's Park Lane town house. It was an intimate sitting room cum library, renovated in the previous century and owing its particular name to the famed designer of the elaborate plasterwork upon its walls and ceilings that featured griffins and winged dragons over a yellow background. Matching decorative stucco framed the windows, the carved marble chimneypiece and a collection of family portraits. Mr. Carysfort was leaning against the marble mantle, twirling a snifter of brandy in one hand, a formidable expression similar to that of the plaster dragon's upon his face.

"Yes, off to see a ballet dancer. That's what he told me." Mr. Carysfort didn't like this development, not in the least. Last night at the Anglesea ball, he could have sworn his nephew had been on the verge of declaring himself to Lady Sarah. What had transpired to change that? This morning, the younger gentleman had awakened in a prodigiously foul humor and had announced his departure to Mr. Carysfort without bothering to say farewell to the ladies or to inform anyone when he might return.

"But this is terrible. Horrible. Dreadful." Lady Ophelia's voice rose to a veritable wail. Giving the sleeves of her velvet gown several nervous yanks, she managed to set the gown askew. She tried to straighten it, failed, and as if overcome by some greater force, she fell back into the velvet covered chair. "Oh, Max, what do you suppose is happening? I thought everything was going so well."

He gave the lady's assessment a few moment's consideration. "That may be the problem. It may be that Beverly found himself entertaining such honorable thoughts about Sarah that he's frightened himself off and has sought escape from himself."

"Is that good or bad?" She gave the sleeves of her gown several more yanks. The dress remained askew.

"I suppose that depends how Sarah feels about him and how she reacts to his absence," Mr. Carysfort said with an inflection that implied he expected Lady Ophelia to speculate upon Sarah's possible response to the earl's rather rude and certainly inexplicable behavior.

"If you expect to learn anything from me you're sadly mistaken. I'm hardly a conduit to my niece's innermost thoughts. Sarah is as silent as ever on the subject of Radnor, and despite my attempts to draw her out, I've been unable to ascertain anything more than that she found the Anglesea ball not so distasteful after all and that Radnor wouldn't let her have a second dance with Conyngham."

"Thank God for that!" Mr. Carysfort raised his snifter as if saluting his nephew's good judgment.

"I agree, but Radnor can be rather domineering, y'know. Perhaps he didn't handle the situation as tactfully as he might have, and they've had a nasty row of the irreparable sort."

"Let's not jump to any hasty conclusions. Who knows what may happen when we return to Hampton Court? I grant you this has all the characteristics of a setback, but I suggest we give it another day or so before donning mourning colors."

Mr. Carysfort's attempted humor failed to produce even the thinnest smile upon Lady Ophelia's lips. "How do you know he'll come back to the palace?"

"I don't, but we mustn't give up, my sweet. And it's not just for ourselves either. Sarah should wed and despite her overnight success—which I'm certain shall yield a bounty of suitors—I stick by my belief that Beverly is the gentleman for her. Likewise I can imagine no other young lady who would better suit Bev. Perhaps the time has come to employ a little subterfuge."

"You mustn't suggest such a thing. I couldn't deceive Sarah." She pinned an indignant glare upon Mr. Carysfort, but his responding expression caused her to feel decidedly uncertain about the proper balance between maintaining her scruples and achieving her future happiness. Her lower lip trembled.

Observing her distress, Mr. Carysfort crossed to stand beside the velvet chair. He leaned to kiss Lady Ophelia upon the forehead. "I didn't mean to upset you, my sweet."

"This must work out. It must." She gazed up at him, a hint of tears in her eyes, and she gave him a wobbly smile. "I cannot bear to live without you, Max, nor can I bear the thought of marrying you, if it means leaving Sarah on her own. What ever are we to do?"

"Don't fret, my sweetest love." He took her hand in his. "It shall work out. I promise we shall be man and wife, if not by the Season's end, then by summer's end. I swear it. Now give me a smile."

Lady Ophelia complied, and they slipped into a companionable silence.

"Hello, you turtle doves," Sarah greeted as she crossed the threshold a few minutes later. She was wearing another one of Madame Tizou's creations, a gown of ivory Indian muslin accented with silver stripes of fine drawnwork and trimmed about the hem and shoulders with a profusion of tinsel leaves. While it was neither as ethereal nor as trend-setting as the amethyst silk ball gown, the lines of the ivory muslin gown were suitably flattering. Sarah, appearing to be swathed as a wood nymph, was a delicate and alluring sight.

"You look lovely, my dear," greeted Lady Ophelia. "And how tidy your hair is. That new style is most flattering."

Sarah thanked her aunt and added, "I'm sorry to have kept you waiting, but this time it wasn't entirely my fault. I was with your mother," she informed Mr. Carysfort. Upon their meeting at breakfast that morning, Sarah had owned an immediate affinity for the witty Dowager Countess of Radnor. The lady still possessed the same light-hearted outlook she'd had as a young woman, and it was easy to see from whence Mr. Carysfort and the earl derived their humor. In addition, Sarah and the elderly lady shared a fondness for history, and Sarah had spent the better part of the day regaling the dowager countess with tales of the hauntings at Hampton Court and the hazards associated with ghost hunting, including, of course, the tale of the netted earl, a story that had caused tears of unbridled merriment to streak down the lady's wrinkled cheeks.

"And how is mother faring, this evening?" Mr. Carysfort remained perched upon the arm of Lady Ophelia's chair, and while he no longer held her hand, he had draped an arm about her shoulder. "Is she obeying the good doctor or did she put up a monumental fuss?"

Sarah laughed. "Your mother is most anxious for her gout to subside in time to attend Lady Russborough's. The dowager countess is a distinctly impatient patient, and were it not for Dr. Bellamy's insistence, she might very well be gadding about this evening."

"Well, at least it's nothing more entertaining than the opera. Mother's never been wild about it, and she won't feel quite so left out."

"On the contrary, sir, she told me she's devastated to miss the display in the pit and has made me promise to report all of the goings-on."

"Ah, yes, sounds like Mother. Did she make a wager?"

"Not with me, but with Dr. Bellamy. A pound that some gentleman by the name of Wattlington shall become so undone by the ruckus that he'll toss at least one of his shoes into the pit."

Mr. Carysfort threw back his head and laughed. "And Mother, I wager, shall on the morrow be a pound plumper."

"Really, Max, you must not give Sarah the impression the opera is little better a three-ringed circus."

There was a humorous glimmer in the gentleman's eye. "No, I shan't. We shall, of course, trust Sarah to arrive at her own conclusion in that matter."

Sarah observed this amiable repartee between her aunt and Mr. Carysfort. There was something comforting about watching the pair of them; there was also something disheartening about it. Of a sudden, she was reminded of the proverbial beggar child standing outside the bun shop window and ogling trays of mouth-watering treats that would always be out of reach. Feeling oddly deprived, Sarah glanced about the Adam's Room. "At least I'm not the only one to have kept you waiting. Where's Lord Radnor?"

An anxious glance, unseen by Sarah, passed between Lady Ophelia and Mr. Carysfort.

"Well, my dear," Lady Ophelia began cautiously, "it seems he won't be joining us this evening."

"Some sort of previous business at his club," Mr. Carysfort added, thinking there could be no harm in offering a vaguely legitimate excuse. "Of course, he sends his most profound regrets and hopes you'll forgive him for not being able to attend the opera with us."

"Business?" Sarah gave a skeptical little laugh. "I must confess to a touch of jealousy."

Panic contorted Lady Ophelia's features, and Mr. Carysfort's left brow arched skyward. Surely, Sarah didn't know about the ballet dancer.

"Jealousy?" squeaked Lady Ophelia.

"I don't mean to hurt your feelings, Aunt Ophelia, but you know I shall never appreciate the opera as you do, and truth to tell, I'm jealous that Lord Radnor's business—whatever it may be—precludes his having to attend. Would that I might be able to cry off with a similar excuse. I'm not used to these late hours and would be more than happy to spend the evening curled up with a book. But as that's not to be the case and since I promised to report every detail to the dowager countess, I'm ready to depart and pledge to try to appreciate the opera for something more than a three-ringed circus," Sarah concluded with a grin, then turned back through the door and headed toward the vestibule where the footman was waiting to drape a cloak about her shoulders.

As they rose to follow Sarah, Lady Ophelia and Mr. Carysfort whispered between themselves.

"At least, she's not angry with him," he said.

"But shouldn't she be disappointed?" she wondered.

Mr. Carysfort shrugged. "One would think so, but far be it for me to presume to comprehend the workings of any female mind." He paused in the corridor to drop another kiss upon Lady Ophelia's forehead. "Now you must promise to put this from your thoughts for the remainder of the evening. We're off to the opera, my sweet. This is your night, and you're going to have a splendid time."

The King's Theatre or the Royal Italian Opera House as it was called by more serious opera devotees was located in the Haymarket. It was the largest theater in England with five tiers of boxes, a pit and gallery, the sum of which could accommodate upwards of three thousand persons, and this evening, every seat was taken. *On dit* Senora Rosetti's performance in the trouser's role of Cherubino, the young messenger, would surpass even the great Catalini, and no one wished to miss an event that might impact on the course of fashion in Society. If Rosetti were destined to eclipse Catalini, every one wished to be able to say, *I was there*, and woe to the individual who would be forced on the morrow to sit in silence while others pontificated upon their firsthand recollections.

Mr. Carysfort escorted the ladies to Lady Ophelia's box, and the trio took their seats as the conductor waved his baton and the opening chords of Mozart's light-hearted overture echoed through the great horseshoe auditorium. Lady Ophelia's box was on the left, nearest to the stage in the second tier, and it afforded a perfect view of the performers as well as most of the other boxes and the pit upon which Sarah focused her attention.

The sight below Sarah was as disorderly as the dowager countess had predicted. Indeed, as Mr. Carysfort had described, it was somewhat akin to a carnival. Several score of over-dressed fops and dandies were making a great nuisance of themselves by strolling about to show off their finely tailored clothes. There was much rattling of ivory and gold-tipped canes, opening and closing of enamel snuff boxes, and a buzz of chatter that persisted even when Senora Rosetti began her first aria. The incessant noise continued through numerous comic hoodwinkings of the countess and Susanna, Lady Ophelia gave an irked sigh, and in an adjoining box a young man called out, "Silence in the pit!" Several other persons echoed this sentiment, and as shouts were exchanged between the tiers and pit Sarah peered about the darkened theater in search of an elderly gentleman aiming a shoe at the ruckus below.

At a box half-way round the horseshoe on the third tier her search was halted by a most unexpected sight. There was the Earl of Radnor sitting bold as brass with a female companion. He wasn't at his club, nor was he attending to business unless his definition of business included auburn-haired women in forest green satin. Even in the dimly lit opera hall, Sarah saw that the lady possessed a striking beauty. Her eyes had an exotic upward slant, her olive-tinted complexion hinted of foreign blood, and the shocking décolletage of her gown revealed an abundant figure. Sarah's first instinct was to look away. Somehow catching sight of the earl in this way seemed like spying, yet she was unable to do anything other than watch in fascination as the auburn-haired woman pressed up against his shoulder and whispered close to his ear; the earl smiled at whatever it was she'd said, and Sarah, to her absolute horror, knew a painful stab of jealousy.

Stunned and confused by this reaction, Sarah closed her eyes and dropped her head. She had no right to such a sentiment. None at all. Logic, however, did not prevail as jealousy turned to hurt. The earl had betrayed their charade. That was why the sight of him with that woman was so troubling, and there was nothing more to her strangely emotional reaction than that. *Nothing at all*, she told herself as she opened her eyes to stare at the beaded reticule upon her lap. Her hands trembled as one particular thought repeated itself in her mind. She had trusted him, and he had betrayed that trust. Well, thank goodness she never succumbed to tears, she mused with a thin shred of humor, or she might be crying buckets right now. Thank goodness, too, she was not a man, or she would be forced to call him out for such dishonorable behavior.

"Damn," the earl swore beneath his breath as he fought to maintain the forced smile upon his lips. What a fool he'd been to imagine he might be able to hide from Lady Sarah, and even though it wasn't his idea to be here, he'd been a bigger fool to allow Louise to force him to escort her. Louise had pouted and flounced and pleaded for more than two hours to no avail, but her threat to go with Viscount Lancing had met with immediate success. Lancing was a braggart and a liar, and the prospect of losing Louise to someone of such base character was galling. In hindsight, Radnor saw how she had manipulated his ego. He was a perfect idiot, but knowing that did not make up for poor judgment, nor could it erase the unhappiness he'd just seen upon Lady Sarah's face.

Perhaps Sarah hadn't seen him, he feebly tried to convince himself. It was exceedingly dark in the opera hall, but not dark enough his conscience argued. Mayhap something else had upset the lady, he speculated casting about for any plausible explanation. But it was pointless. The earl knew there was no avoiding the fact that he'd treated Lady Sarah shabbily. Despite his promise to stay by her side and support their charade, he had quit the town house without a word of explanation only to be discovered in the company of a woman whose reputation as a ballet dancer was equal only to her fame as a demi-rep. What a hypocrite he was. While he had purported to protect Lady Sarah from the tabbies at the Anglesea ball, he had quite neatly managed to give them plenty to talk about this night.

"Louise, must you sit so close?" he demanded in a testy voice. "I thought you wished to see the opera. If you wished to make love, we could have stayed home and done so without all the world to see."

"Please, my lord," the auburn-haired exotic purred. "Do not be angry." She straightened up, but allowed her hand to linger on his inner thigh. "I only wish to please you."

"Well, public displays don't please me," he shot back. "They never have."

Louise affected a dreadful pout, wondering what it was that had put his lordship in such a state. It was probably another woman, she deduced, her eyes moving about the theater in search of her rival.

Who might it be? Lord Suffolk had been wounded in a duel last week, and *on dit* Deirdre Brighton was casting about for a new protector. Louise followed the direction of the earl's gaze. He was staring at a box in the tier below. There, Louise recognized the earl's uncle, Mr. Carysfort with two ladies, and being an avid reader of the daily announcements in the *Post*, she assumed the older lady was his fiancé.

Turning a quick glance toward the earl was sufficient for Louise to ascertain that it was the other lady, the younger one with masses of pale gold hair, who commanded his lordship's attention. She was lovely, but Louise was not jealous. She was after all a lady, and ladies and wives were no threat to an experienced woman of the *demi-monde*. What disturbed Louise was the obvious misery upon the young lady's face.

"Now I understand your reluctance to bring me this evening, my lord," she said offering the earl an understanding smile. Neither her expression nor her voice contained a trace of reproach. The earl did not reply, and Louise, knowing precisely how to handle a man, allowed him several moments cogitation before she posed a gentle query, "Does the young lady deserve an apology, my lord?"

"Not for the reasons you may suspect." His gaze did not waver from Lady Sarah, who was looking every which way except in his direction.

Several more moments of silence ensued. On more than one occasion, Louise had managed to convince even the most guarded gentleman to confide his inner-most secrets, and now she put her skills to the test. "I think what you are telling me is that there is

no tendre between yourself and that young lady."
He nodded in the affirmative. "For what reason then
would you apologize?"

"We shared a common goal—to avoid matrimony—and we had a bargain of sorts to insure that
goal. We were to feign a courtship, and in doing so
I was to thwart her aunt's matchmaking intentions
while she would protect me from marriage-minded
debutantes."

"Ah, now I understand." Louise grinned at the
brilliance of their bargain. If it were to prevent
the earl from marrying, it suited her own interests as well. "If only you had told me earlier, my
lord, I would not have been such a selfish creature
to make you come out this evening. Perhaps you
should visit the young lady during the intermission
and set matters to right."

"So I shall," he said staring at Lady Sarah and
willing her to glance in his direction. He wished
to see her expression and to reassure himself that
the pain and confusion he had earlier seen upon
her delicate features had vanished. But when she
finally looked up he was far from reassured, for
she appeared to be flirting with the skill of an
experienced coquette.

Preventing her eyes from straying to the earl was
no easy task for Sarah. The temptation to steal a
peek at him was overwhelming, and each time she
knew the urge to turn in his direction, she forced
herself to practice the flirtatious wiles she had seen
other young ladies perform. There was Sir Benjamin on the other side of the theater; she returned
his nod with a brilliant smile. Lord Conyngham
stared at her; she returned his bold gaze over the

scalloped edge of her fan. And when a foxed young gentleman dared to offer her a drunken salute she acknowledged him as well.

The curtain fell on the first act, and Lord Radnor leapt to his feet to depart Louise's box. What was wrong with Lady Sarah? Had one night on the Town turned her into a vain coquette? This sort of behavior was the last thing he would have expected from her. In fact, there was something almost defiant about the lady he decided as he made his way toward the staircase.

By the time he reached Lady Ophelia's box, there was already a veritable crush of gentlemen come to pay their respects, and for several moments, the earl was forced to stand in a corner from which he observed the goings-on. Lady Sarah was exquisite. Even more so than last evening, for tonight there was a new radiance about her, a sort of glowing palpable female allure. It was enticing and enchanting, and Radnor wasn't sure whether he really liked what he saw. The truth was he rather missed the Lady Sarah he had come to admire, the Lady Sarah with the disorderly hair whose haphazard style was not so perfect or engaging. Like a cup of nectar Lady Sarah was surrounded by gentlemen who reminded Radnor of a mass of hungry bees, and Sir Benjamin sporting a canary yellow waistcoat was the hungriest of the buzzing creatures.

From his corner, Radnor heard Sir Benjamin reissue his invitation for a ride in the park, and for one awful instant the earl was seized by the fear that Lady Sarah might actually accept. Pushing his way to Sarah's side, he responded before she might speak for herself.

"Lady Sarah and I are returning to Hampton Court first thing in the morning. We must get back to our work. Mustn't we, my dear?"

Sarah felt as if the breath had been knocked from her lungs. Where had Lord Radnor come from? And what right did he have to be so odiously domineering? *He* was supposed to be courting her, or at least, creating that impression, and attending the opera in another lady's company was most counterproductive. Sweet heaven, he confused her, and while she wished to deliver a swift kick to his shins, she also wished to fall into his arms. There was, however, no time to sort out her emotions, and only one instinct—her fierce pride—guided her as she gazed up at him with a dazzling smile.

She stood on tiptoe, raised her fan and spoke close to his ear. "Someday you must tell me about your *business obligations*, sir. I'm sure they're fascinating."

Her smile never wavered, nor did his as he replied to a question from one of the other gentlemen in the box. This little scene elicited an audible sigh of relief from Lady Ophelia. It appeared the setback in their romance had been temporary and the courtship was back on course, and she shared a secret glance with Mr. Carysfort whose expression confirmed this assessment.

All observers of the goings-on in Lady Ophelia's box were not, however, pleased by what they saw. From the next tier, Louise peered through her opera glasses and frowned; she regretted the generous impulse to suggest Lord Radnor visit the young lady. While Mr. Carysfort, Lady Ophelia and the Countess of Mornington may have thought

Radnor and Lady Sarah were suited, Louise was the first to realize the truth. To one knowledgeable in matters of seduction and romance it was obvious: the pair was madly in love.

12

"THERE ARE FEW settings more conducive to romance than a leisurely boat ride," Lady Ophelia had explained to Mr. Carysfort when he had vented a series of disgruntled oaths upon learning they were to make the return journey to Hampton Court via barge. The boat trip was a strategy Lady Ophelia had devised to nourish the fledgling romance between Sarah and the earl, and she did not wish Mr. Carysfort to put a damper on it. It was of the utmost importance that he temper his attitude.

In the end, Mr. Carysfort obliged, but Lord Radnor and Sarah did not.

"Yes, my lord, your betrayal," Sarah hissed in a high state of annoyance. She and the earl were seated on a cushion-strewn dais beneath a blue and white canopy in the center of the barge as it floated up the Thames. At the bow, Lady Ophelia and Mr. Carysfort were investigating the contents of a picnic hamper, and while Sarah did not wish to disturb them with sounds of a quarrel there was much she wished to say to the earl about his conduct at the opera. Having given the matter much consideration, she supposed his odiously domineering attitude could be chalked up to their charade, but by no stretch of the imagination was there any reasonable explanation for his having appeared in the company of another woman, and a woman whom Sarah suspected was a *demi mondaine*. She was emphatic, "Yes, your betrayal, my lord. That's what you did. You betrayed our agreement, and it's wrong of you to put a different face on it."

"And I think you're overreacting," retorted the earl. "Painting it a tad too brown, don't you think?"

"Don't you dare take that condescending tone with me." Sarah's angry voice was matched by the expression upon her face. The color of her eyes had deepened to a dark purple and her lips were pursed into a tight little pucker. "I'm being honest with you, sir, and in kind you should not seek to minimize the impropriety of your actions last evening."

"Well, it's not as if we were married," he rejoined assuming a somewhat petulant tenor.

Sarah glared at him in stony silence. Behind them a boatman manned the tiller while another man poled the craft toward its destination, and the only noise that broke the awkward silence between Sarah and the earl was the hollow plop of the boatman's pole each time it entered the swirling river. At length, she agreed, "No, it's not as if we were married." Some of the anger faded from her voice. "And please understand that I'm not presuming to say what you should do with your time or with whom. I'm merely reminding you that we made an agreement which you betrayed and in doing so disappointed me deeply."

In a revealing gesture the earl raked his fingers through his hair. He was not accustomed to such honesty from a female, particularly when it featured him the culprit. It made him exceedingly nervous. "You tell me nothing I haven't already told myself, Lady Sarah. And I apologize. I was thoughtless and selfish, and there's no excuse for what I did."

Had the earl tried to justify his behavior with some flimsy explanation, Sarah would have been furious. His apology alone satisfied her, and she offered a tentative smile. "Your apology is accepted. Now you must tell me, sir, do you still wish to continue our charade?"

"Of course. My opinions on matrimony haven't changed. And how about you, Lady Sarah, have your notions changed?"

"Why would you even wonder?" She tilted her head to peer at him from beneath the brim of her chip bonnet.

"You were the object of so much attention while in Town I thought perhaps . . ."

"My head had been turned? Hardly." Her smile warmed and the color in her eyes lightened. "In point of fact, you were right to warn me that Sir Benjamin and Lord Conyngham were considering me solely on the basis of how I might benefit their individual interests. And how horrid and depressing it is to realize that neither gentleman cared one jot for who I might be or what sort of interests I might own. That alone sustains my belief that I must avoid matrimony at all cost." She gave a sad sort of sigh. "What a dismal thing marriage must be for so many young ladies. My heart goes out to them. To relinquish so much with nothing in return, not even a sympathetic ear."

Lady Sarah's words deeply moved the earl. To his dismay, they conjured up an image of this ebullient young woman wasting away in loneliness, exiled to a husband's country seat and denied all opportunity to explore the world about her. Such a thought was unmentionable, and the earl shook his head as if to clear this vision from his mind's eye. He required several moments before he might speak. "Then we shall proceed as before?"

"Naturally. And not only for myself, but for you as well, my lord. Despite your transgression, you did make my first night in London a painless one, and I could do no less than continue, particularly since you're liable to have a visit from Lady Charlotte at any time."

"Good lord, do you really think so?"

Her smile relaxed into a full grin. "I believe your grandmother would consider it a sound wager."

He emitted a theatrical groan, and Sarah responded with a light ripple of laughter. It was good to relegate their troubles to the past and go on as before. The first thought Sarah had had upon waking this morning had been a most unfortunate stab of regret that things might have changed between herself and the earl. Quite unexpectedly, she had come to enjoy his company; perhaps, she confessed to herself, even to look forward to it, and she was not prepared to give it up. Too soon the Season would end and the earl would go off to Temple Radnor. For the time being, she did not wish to dwell upon that day; she wished to enjoy as much of his company as was possible.

They settled into a companionable silence. The tide was favorable this day, and the barge was nearing the halfway point in the journey up the Thames. Having been afloat for an hour, they had left behind the noise and pollution of the metropolis, and as they passed Kew the river ran silver clear.

Sarah was the first to speak. "Would you be scandalized if I took off my bonnet?"

"Not in the least. The day's become dreadfully hot. You must go ahead."

She set the bonnet at her feet, and then as if it were the most natural thing in the world she gave her head a gentle shake to cool herself. Several pale curls tumbled about her face and an errant flaxen wisp clung to one cheek presenting an altogether intoxicating sight. Deftly, her fingers tousled the curls achieving no order but creating a tiny cooling breeze about her neck, and as the earl watched this he was certain he could detect the faint scent of early spring roses.

Desire rose within him like a high tide on the full moon, and he swallowed in a dry throat before he could inquire, "Are we to continue our charade under the same ground rules as before?"

"Sir?"

"That I must not touch you."

Crimson dots colored Sarah's cheeks, and she glanced away. For several heartbeats she stared at the passing shoreline where two small boys sat with fishing poles and strings of sunfish. "Do you think it's necessary? *Touching*?"

He couldn't help grinning. Her discomposure was positively enchanting. "There might be one or two situations in which some carefully orchestrated contact might be acceptable. Relationships do change, you know, and what could have seemed excessive earlier on might be natural now."

"Oh," was the best she could manage. "There might?"

He gave an affirming nod.

"And is now one of those times?" she asked with an horrendous stutter.

"Nothing too drastic. I merely think we should endeavor to appear more like Max and Lady Ophelia."

Sarah glanced toward the bow where her aunt and Mr. Carysfort were seated beneath an oversized parasol. They presented a perfect picture of lovers reclining against a bank of chintz cushions; Aunt Ophelia was nestled against Mr. Carysfort's shoulder and his chin rested in familiar fashion upon the top of her head. They looked quite blissful, and observing this, Sarah again experienced a strange feeling as if something precious was just out of her reach. Her voice fell to an oddly husky whisper, "That's all?"

"That's all," he said, knowing how easily an innocent situation could deepen into something far more intimate. She whispered her assent, and the corners of his mouth arched into a roguish grin. "That's very wise of you, Lady Sarah. Very wise, indeed." Without further ado, he patted the cushion beside him and held open his arm in an inviting pose. Slowly, Sarah inched into the space he had made for her. Once she was settled by his side, they sat for several minutes neither daring to move.

"Shall we see what cook has packed in our hamper?" he suggested in a voice that reminded Sarah of velvet.

She exhaled a pent-up breath. "Please," she replied anxious for anything that might divert her mind from her startling awareness of the earl. This had looked quite harmless, but, in truth, he was far too close. She could hear his heart, smell a pleasant male sort of scent that reminded her of sandalwood and pine needles, and she could feel the overwhelming masculine hardness of his chest. Sorting through the picnic basket was not, however, the sobering diversion she had hoped it would be. Rather with every motion the earl made Sarah became more and more aware of the way his arm and chest muscles flexed as he set out an assortment of fruits and cheeses and pastries. So tantalizing was this assault on her senses that she forgot all about the charade and succumbed to the temptation to close her eyes and lose herself in an intimate awareness of his strength. She knew she shouldn't be sitting like this, eyes closed and concentrating on his rippling muscles; she shouldn't be wondering what it might feel like to cup her palm about his bare arm; nor should she be enjoying the wobbly, faint-headed way it made her feel. There was something utterly wanton about it. Unforgivably wanton.

The earl held a small piece of cheese to her lips and she ate it, her lips momentarily brushing against his fingers. She shivered. "I think we're being dreadfully wicked."

"That's what some might call this." With his free hand he managed to pour a glass of wine and hand it to her. "Do you feel damned for eternity?"

She indulged in a rather too lengthy sip of wine. "A bit. It's sort of like standing on the edge of a cliff with the wind tugging at me, trying to pull me into a whirlpool. Does that sound strange?"

"Not really." He recalled his earliest rushes of sensual pleasure and knew that was what Sarah was describing. A combined rush of longing and protectiveness crashed over him, for while he wished to crush her to him and teach her the joys of passion between a man and a woman, he knew he couldn't do so. She had no notion what was happening to her and he would not be the one to destroy her innocence.

"Is this what cyprians do?" she wondered aloud.

"Good lord, Lady Sarah, what do you know of such things?"

"Not much except that I always pitied them for depending on men. But if this is what they do, mayhap I was too quick to judge, and in truth, their lives are pleasurable after all." She took another sip of wine. "Do you think it would be better to be a wife or a cyprian?"

"Lady Sarah, you must not even consider such a thing!" he was genuinely horrified.

"It must be the wine. I fear it's gone to my head."

"Yes." He took the empty wine glass from her and set it aside.

"Please, you must excuse me. I'm suddenly rather tired, my lord." She stifled a yawn. "Town life is exhausting, isn't it? It was fun, but I'm glad to be returning home."

He wasn't sure why, but he liked to hear Lady Sarah say those words. *Returning home.* It was certainly safer than talking about cyprians. He patted her hand and drew her closer. "If you like, close your eyes and rest. You may pretend I'm a giant pillow."

"What a splendid idea." This time she did not prevent the yawn. "We shall be busy this coming week with the final stages of the work at the Old Court House. A nap would be very nice, indeed."

They had planned several vigils at the old Court House, and although the earl knew they would be passed in silence, he was looking forward to those hours of solitude with Lady Sarah. "And after the Old Court House what do you plan? Another vigil for Queen Jane?"

"I'm not sure yet." She closed her eyes and fell silent. Several moments passed, and it was neither the lapping of waves against the hull nor the call of gulls overhead that Sarah heard but his heartbeat, reminding her how vitally masculine he was and how close they were. It was almost as if they were one, and Sarah wished this moment might never end. "Do you really find my work as interesting as you professed to Lady Charlotte?"

"It wasn't a fabrication to put off Lady Charlotte, if that's what you thought. While I did intend to bore her, I spoke the truth. Your work is refreshing and unique. You explore notions that push the boundaries of reality to their limit, and I find that intriguing. It's rather like exercise for the mind. Heretofore, I was singularly devoted to athletic endeavors, but, a fit body is rather useless without a fit mind, y'know."

"How glad I am to hear you say that," she mumbled as she drifted to sleep in the cradle of his arms. "Very glad, my lord. Very glad."

The barge continued up river, children's laughter echoed from the shore, and Radnor watched Sarah. It was a good thing their foray into Town had come to an end. Any more moments like those at the Anglesea ball or in Lady Ophelia's box at the opera and he was bound to be standing before a magistrate on charges of first degree murder. The thought of Sir Benjamin and Conyngham made his blood seethe, and the worst of it was they weren't the only scoundrels waiting to take advantage of a lady as innocent and trusting as Lady Sarah. London was filled with their type, and Radnor was determined she should be protected from them. He would make it his business to guarantee she didn't return to Town. He'd do whatever was necessary to keep her at Hampton Court until the Season ended, and she was once again safe from Lady Ophelia's matrimonial schemes.

A gust of wind blew a strand of flaxen hair over her eyes. Gently, he brushed it away, allowing his fingertips to rest against her soft warm skin as he lowered his lips to linger upon her cheek in a tender caress that revealed emotions his conscious mind had yet to realize.

13

B Y THE WEEK'S end, Sarah had concluded the second and third stages of the investigation in the Old Court House. She had interviewed the gardener and household staff, studied the late afternoon light patterns in the dining room and corridor, and sat vigil with the earl for three nights, arriving at the conclusion that the disturbances were more likely a result of the cook's secret indulgence in Portuguese sherry than any supernatural visitation. Major Lord Hugh and Lady MacGregor returned to their home, whereupon the cook retired to her bed with a mysterious malaise, and Sarah decided to wait several weeks before continuing to explore that particular site. Besides she needed to catch up on paperwork, and to her astonishment, the earl was more than willing to assist in that tedious task.

One week turned to a second and then a third as they spent their mornings seated on the floor in Lady Ophelia's drawing room sorting through copies of various presentations before the Royal Society which they read aloud to one another, then discussed and debated at length. Each afternoon before tea, they strolled through the palace gardens, on one occasion tackling the Maze located in the ten acre Wilderness, and at other times merely enjoying the path through the cool-scented grove of lime trees toward the river on the East Front; sometimes Lady Ophelia and Mr. Carysfort accompanied them, well pleased that the younger couple had begun to hold hands and often conversed in intimate whispered tones.

For Sarah, those mornings spent in work and those afternoons in the gardens with the earl were like a chapter out of a novel in which everyone was blissfully happy and nothing was of greater importance than the moment at hand. By choice, her circle of friends was small, and had anyone suggested that a gentleman such as the Earl of Radnor might rank among them she would have balked; now he was an integral part of her daily life. There was a mutual respect between them, a shared sense of the absurd, and something quite extraordinary about the way he made her feel which was very female and more than a little vulnerable. From Sarah's perspective none of this had anything to do with their charade. Somehow their relationship had assumed a form of its own, but she didn't know whether the earl shared this opinion, and she dared not inquire, for she feared that to do so might cause him to take flight from Hampton Court as he had from London.

As for the earl, those days with Sarah were a combination of heaven and hell. Heavenly, that their charade allowed him those hours in her presence. Usually, his interludes with females were brief and devoted to matters other than conversation. The course of his relationship with Lady Sarah was bewildering. Never before had he enjoyed female company as he did Lady Sarah's. At first, he attributed this phenomenon to the fact that he could be in a lady's company without worrying about her motivations, but soon he realized the source of his pleasure was in the lady herself. She was, indeed, everything a gentleman could wish for. She was sweet and generous, forthright and honorable, intelligent and witty, beautiful and innocent, and his earlier urge to protect her from all unworthy gentlemen fast increased. Verily, he came to include himself among that misbegotten crew, for his own desire to kiss her, nay make passionate love to her, swelled until it neared a flashpoint, and each time she innocently slipped her hand in his there ensued a mammoth struggle between his conscience and his lustier self to keep his passion at bay. Indeed, so great was that struggle that he feared he might have to return to Louise.

Of course, none of this was known to Lady Ophelia or Mr. Carysfort, who, by the third week following the opera, was growing increasingly disturbed by the comfortable appearance of the friendship between Sarah and the earl. So careful were each of the young people to disguise their true emotions that they reminded Mr. Carysfort of a married couple, who after several decades of a *mariage de convenance* had achieved a pleasant understanding. Thus it was that the use of subterfuge became a frequent subject of dispute between Mr. Carysfort and Lady Ophelia. The gentleman spoke in favor of it, the lady against it. Then in the first week of June, an event occurred which tipped the scales in Mr. Carysfort's favor. The earl quit Hampton Court.

Swooning into the arms of the Earl of Radnor had become *de rigueur* in the Chapel Royal. On three consecutive Sundays, he was subjected to theatrical displays of the fragile female constitution. It began with Lady Charlotte who, as Sarah had predicted, took the first available opportunity to visit the palace and managed to twist her ankle at the communion rail; next Miss Camilla tried where her twin had failed, enjoying an equal lack of success when Mr. Carysfort, in lieu of the earl, volunteered to escort her to the yard for a breath of fresh air; and finally, a relative of Miss Wellesley's fiancé collapsed at the earl's feet in the middle of the aisle as if overcome by the very sight of his masculine personage.

To the majority of grace and favor residents it seemed a rather natural outcome to this appalling series of incidents that the earl did not attend services on the fourth Sunday. Hardly caring where he might have taken himself, they were simply gratified that the gentleman had done something to put a halt to the shameful scenes. Mr. Carysfort, however, viewed his absence in a wholly different light.

"Something ain't right," he declared to Lady Ophelia as they exited the chapel that Sunday morning. Sarah, who was walking several paces behind them, had stopped to chat with the Reverend Wellesley.

"Of course, something isn't right," Lady Ophelia concurred. "The poor fellow's been plagued by those odious females. Any gentleman in his right mind would stay away. To my mind, it shows a remarkable degree of self-control that Radnor chose to absent himself rather than throttle those preposterous creatures."

"He isn't merely staying away, my sweet, he's left for London. Gone off to see that ballet dancer again," Mr. Carysfort stated in a funereal tone, and Lady Ophelia's hand flew to her breast in dismay. The gentleman continued, "I tell you none of this budding-romance folderol rings true, and we should've done something to bring matters to a conclusion long before now."

Lady Ophelia was forced to agree. She and Mr. Carysfort had wished to see romance blossom between their younger relatives, hence that was what they had seen. The truth, however, was a very different story, and when Tuesday morning dawned without the earl's return, Lady Ophelia, unwilling to abandon the notion of a match between Sarah and the earl, took the unprecedented step of seeking Lady Mornington's counsel.

"My dear girl, you needn't make excuses for talking to me of this," the countess assured Lady Ophelia. The day was overcast, and they sat before a window overlooking the countess's garden, a galleried table with frosted scones and a China-trade tea service positioned between them. "I'm more than happy to help, but first you must tell me what's transpired to make you so Friday-faced. I can't believe the situation's entirely hopeless." After listening for several minutes, the older woman was persuaded to set her teacup on the table and question, "You don't suppose it was a ruse, do you?"

"I don't follow, ma'am."

"That the signs of romance were feigned. That, perhaps, for reasons known only to themselves, Sarah and Radnor agreed to be in one another's company and make it appear as if a tendre were developing between them."

Lady Ophelia cogitated upon this theory. "That would account for the lack of development."

"Precisely, and having discerned what's truly going on, it only remains for you to decide what's to be done," the countess declared.

"If anything's to be done at all," Lady Ophelia rejoined in a wholly dispirited tone. She had had such high expectations for the future—for herself and Max, and for Sarah and Radnor—now none of it seemed possible. "Do you think I'm wrong Lady Mornington? I thought they were suited."

"You're not wrong, my dear. They are suited. Saw it myself that morning they came to call. Y'know, it isn't often I meddle in other people's affairs, but when two young persons can't see the truth as plain as their noses then it's the responsibility of those older and wiser to show them."

"I'm relieved to hear you say that, ma'am." Lady Ophelia smiled for the first time since Mr. Carysfort had told her about the earl's departure. "Max says we should concoct some sort of ploy to force the issue."

"Sounds rather over-zealous for Mr. Carysfort. Since when did he start taking an interest in his nephew's future?"

"Since I put a condition on our betrothal."

"Shame on you, Lady Ophelia." The countess leaned forward to rap the younger lady on the knuckles with her lorgnette. "Why ever did you do such a foolhardy thing?"

Lady Ophelia blushed. "At first, I told myself it was because I didn't wish to leave Sarah on her own, but now—as I face the prospect of not marrying Max—I know it's because I don't wish Sarah to make the same mistake as myself. While my life hasn't been entirely wasted there has been a certain bareness to it, and I don't want Sarah to pass another fifteen or twenty years before she comes to her senses."

The countess chuckled. "Should I live to be a hundred, Lady Ophelia, you will never disappoint me. Very sound reasoning, my dear. Very sound. Now you must continue to please me and heed Mr. Carysfort, for I must agree that some scheme is required. It's no longer merely an issue of Sarah and Radnor. The future happiness of four souls is at stake, and if you don't do something it may soon be too late for all of you."

Although Lady Ophelia did not like the notion of hoodwinking Sarah, she knew that Mr. Carysfort and the countess were correct. "Have you any suggestions, ma'am? I'm not sure whether Lord Radnor even intends to return to the palace."

"Then you must give him a reason to return. He could not refuse to attend a betrothal party for you and Mr. Carysfort, and as you've no relative to hostess such an affair in your behalf I would be honored to do so."

"That is most generous of you, ma'am."

"Generous! I'll not hear such fustian. You'd be doing me a great favor, my dear girl. I need something to take my mind off all this talk of war on the Continent. A party's just the ticket."

"You must forgive me, ma'am. How shameful that in my selfishness I've managed to forget your brave son and our troops, and the peril they face."

"More fustian!" The countess waved an impatient hand in the air. "No more talk like that. Arthur would not have us moping about. Always was the most pragmatic of my boys. He would expect me to remain stalwart and unflinchingly normal, and I mustn't let him down."

Lady Ophelia nodded in understanding. "Then I accept your gracious offer. I believe a small dinner fete would suffice. No more than thirty guests, mostly Carysforts, I fear."

"And if we might have it in your apartment rather than mine I believe the palace housekeeper would allow us the use of the adjacent receiving rooms to set out a buffet and dining tables. Of course, I'll attend to the invitations. Just give me a list. You're not to worry about any of the details. I'll provide the flowers and menu and bring along my staff, plus a few extra girls from the village."

"That would be fine, ma'am." Feeling better, Lady Ophelia decided the frosted scones looked rather tasty and she helped herself to one. She swallowed a small bite, then inquired, "And once Radnor is returned what shall we do then, ma'am?"

"The most obvious thing is to have them discovered in a compromising situation by some veritable dragon of the Ton. They shall be discovered the night of the party, and I shall be that dragon."

"But how—?"

The elderly lady raised her lorgnette and scowled down the length of her aristocratic nose. "Don't disappoint me, Lady Ophelia. I was sure your superior imagination was up to this challenge." Lady Ophelia teased her lower lip between her teeth. Several moments passed. The countess poured more tea into the blue and white flowered cups. "Might I suggest that you concentrate on your niece's weakness. Her Achilles' heel as it were. I believe the girl is perpetually late and no doubt shall still be about her toilette long after your guests have arrived for the engagement fete."

Inspiration lit Lady Ophelia's countenance. "And were Radnor to stumble upon her in a state of *déshabillé* we would have the makings of such a scandal that an immediate marriage to protect her reputation would be the sole recourse."

The Countess of Mornington responded with a vigorous nod of endorsement, the details were ironed out, and the plot was launched. A date was set for the dinner fete, a sennight hence; the guest list was finalized and invitations were dispatched. The day of the party arrived as did the guests, the earl among them; and at the appointed moment, Lady Ophelia took a fortifying breath as she approached the earl to beg a favor.

"Would you mind terribly, sir, if I asked you to get my fan? I seem to have left it in my room." As anticipated Lord Radnor agreed, but paused to inquire as to the location of Lady Ophelia's room. "It's the closed door at the end of the corridor," she replied knowing that Sarah's door, not hers, would be closed.

Unlike previous occasions, it was not a book on architectural history or the latest edition of the *Philosophical Transactions* which delayed Sarah this evening. It was the altogether frivolous issue of what to wear. Never before had Sarah been stymied by the simple act of dressing. More often than not, she didn't change her outfit merely because the sun had set, but, if unavoidable, she resorted to grabbing the first reasonably pressed gown in the wardrobe. This night, however, the prospect of the earl's return had submerged her into a most uncharacteristic dither. She had pulled out the first frock—a lilac satin creation by Madame Tizou—and finding it most unsatisfactory, owing to the fact that the earl had already seen her in it, she had pulled out a second dress, then a third, a fourth, and a fifth.

The earl had been gone for little more than a week, yet that time had been an eternity to Sarah who found herself unable to banish the gentleman from her mind. Everything she did or saw reminded her of him, and although she attempted to finish her paperwork, she couldn't. Repeatedly, she had paused to impart a tidbit of curious information to him only to remember he wasn't there. Two days had not passed before an unforeseen loneliness had beset Sarah, not dissimilar to the one she had known during that long voyage to England after her parents's death.

This time, however, there was a difference. Although Aunt Ophelia was always available to listen and counsel, Sarah had been unable to confide in her. There was something shameful about the way the earl made her feel, and she couldn't bear to reveal that shame, not even to Aunt Ophelia.

The earl had left a note:

Dear Lady Sarah, Although it was my intention to assist you until your work's completion, personal business demands my immediate return to the metropolis. Please accept my apology and my suggestion that you reread Dalton's essay on the atomic theory. I'm sure you'll agree that his interpretation of matter is most intriguing.

Yours faithfully, Radnor.

The missive was polite, and it would have been more than sufficient had it not been for Sarah's myriad and persistent insecurities. Had she caused him to leave? Had she displeased him in some way? Was it as the gossips supposed? Hampton Court had ceased to be a refuge from unscrupulous and marriage-minded females. If so, then she had failed him.

During his absence, the notion of making up for this transgression had assumed paramount importance in Sarah's scheme of thought. Now he was returning, and she was determined to please him, which accounted for this ridiculous indecision regarding wardrobe.

Sarah heard the bedchamber door open. "Aunt Ophelia?" Turning to inquire whether the Clarence blue satin suited better than the rose silk, she saw the earl. Standing in the doorway, garbed in formal black, the starched collar of his pristine white shirt brushed against his jaw in perfect contrast to his rugged masculine features. To Sarah, who had longed for his return, he had never seemed so tall or handsome or so irresistibly male. It was

Hermes standing on her threshold. What a beautiful, welcomed sight he was, and a radiant smile illuminated her face. "Lord Radnor, good evening, sir. Oh, how happy I am you are returned at last."

As a gentleman and a peer, the earl knew he should divert his gaze from Sarah and remove himself from the room posthaste. But he was transfixed by the sight of the lady poised over the pile of dresses upon the four poster bed. His gaze moved from her sparkling eyes to the smooth creaminess of her throat where her pulse thudded, then to the gentle swell of bosom and her tiny waist, and finally, to her bare feet peeking from beneath a lacy undergarment. His blood quickened, and his eyes strayed upward once more to the thin fabric hiding her breasts. He heard her say something in a light pleasant tone. She was pleased to see him, he thought with the enthusiasm of a schoolboy, and enchanted by the moment, he couldn't resist asking, "Did you really miss me?"

"Of course." Sarah felt her face grow warm beneath his regard, and her heart contracted. Intuition told Sarah her appearance had shaken the earl, and she found she rather liked that. The color in her cheeks heightened, and of a sudden, she was acutely aware that something had changed between them. Although she knew Radnor would never hurt her, she couldn't help feeling that she wasn't quite safe. His gaze was too direct, his tone too warm, and the situation was frightfully improper. She crossed her arms at the chest and turned to one side.

"Don't tell me you've suddenly become shy." The earl held his breath.

"I believe so," she faltered in her reply.

The proper course was to offer a profound apology and depart without another moment's delay, but Sarah's ingenuous words, and her state of *déshabillé* were more than the earl could handle. He'd been on his best behavior with Sarah, but continued restraint was too much to ask of him, and Radnor couldn't stop himself from crossing the carpet to stand before her. His voice fell to a husky whisper. "You're not afraid of me, are you?"

Less than ten or twelve inches separated them. He towered over Sarah and she'd never been more aware of his potential masculine strength than she was at that moment. She took a tiny step backward and bravely said, "I–I don't think so."

"Only think?" He grinned down at her, his smile was warm and hypnotic. This was the rake speaking now in a slow velvety tone. "Well, then you must let me show you there's nothing to fear." He reached out to gently pull her into an embrace, but she didn't budge. "Come, Sarah," he said, his voice soft and seductive. "There's nothing to fear. I shan't bite, I promise." He took two steps, closing the gap between them, his arms wrapping around her shoulders to hold her against his chest.

Sarah didn't dare move a muscle. "I–I think you should leave now." And then she looked up knowing that if she dared to meet his gaze, he would know she meant what she'd said, but it was a mistake, a fateful miscalculation, for in raising her face she turned upward into his hovering lips. Their mouths brushed, their breaths mingled, her own lips tingled as if on fire, and the earl's reaction to this contact was immediate.

An exquisite agony coursed through Lord Radnor, and he groaned. Her lips were warm and soft, her breath sweet, her tiny form was deliciously soft, and her hair smelled of early roses. Despite the past nights in Louise's company, Radnor still needed Sarah. Her skin begged caressing; her flaxen curls enticed his fingers to thread through them; and those moist ruby lips demanded to be thoroughly kissed. Slipping his hands from her shoulders to her waist, he crushed her to him, and his mouth claimed hers.

All thought of propriety was doused, all thought of resistance was vanquished. Sarah's lips moved beneath the pressure of his, and of their own volition, her arms wound about his shoulders, her hands linking at the nape of his neck. She quivered and pressed closer to him. A harsh sound rose from the depth of his throat, and a sixth sense told Sarah she had pleased the earl. Again, she pressed against the hardness of his thighs and chest.

What began as a gentle kiss soon deepened to one of urgent need. Sarah trembled as his embrace tightened and one of his hands moved upward from her waist and his fingers touched the swell of her breast. She gasped against his lips. She had never felt like this before. Never. This was more dangerous than standing on the edge of the cliff and being tugged by the wind. This was what it was like to plummet from that cliff.

Somewhere in the back of her mind, Sarah heard someone cry out. The sound seemed to be coming from very far away, muted as if insulated by a turban of gauze. The earl must have heard the noise, too, for he lifted his lips from hers. Slowly, her eyelids flickered open, and she stared up at the earl. He was glancing over his shoulder, and she followed his gaze. There upon the threshold, stood the Countess of Mornington, an expression of condemnation etched upon her countenance.

Speaking as if she were both judge and jury, the venerable lady indicted the earl, "Heed well, sirrah. Such license is not without its price."

brew than Lady Sarah . . . circumstances of your
wedding grieve me to . . ." she said between
watery sniffles.

". . . won't go," burst forth the earl as he jumped

14

S ARAH OWNED NO recollection of a more ag-
onizing nor more humiliating interview than the
one to which she was subjected in Mr. Carysfort's
apartment at ten o'clock the following morning. She
and the earl were ordered to take seats on opposite sides of the room, while Lady Ophelia sat on
the gold and maroon striped sofa with her future
mother-in-law the Dowager Countess of Radnor
to her left, her co-conspirator the Countess of
Mornington to the right. Mr. Carysfort, who had
convened the meeting, paced back and forth in the
center of the room, speaking in a stentorian voice
and alternately pointing an accusing finger at his
nephew, then scowling at Sarah.

Lady Mornington confirmed the crime. There was
no doubt as to what she had witnessed in Lady
Sarah's bedchamber. It was scandalous. Disgrace-

ful. Ruinous. The girl's reputation had been well and truly compromised by the earl.

Upon hearing this confirmation, the Dowager Countess of Radnor gazed upon her grandson. Tears welled in her eyes. "While I had almost despaired that you would ever wed, dearest Beverly, and while I could want for no better granddaughter-in-law than Lady Sarah, the circumstances of your wedding grieve me to no end," she said between watery sniffles.

"Our wedding!" burst forth the earl as he jumped to his feet. His horror at his grandmother's statement was echoed in the mute appeal upon Sarah's face as she looked at the trio of ladies on the gold and maroon striped sofa.

"What did you think this meeting was all about?" demanded Mr. Carysfort. He aimed that accusing finger at his nephew. "Sit down, Bev. You aren't going anywhere, not until this is resolved."

"And what do you propose?" queried the earl in a dry tone. He did not sit down as instructed, but crossed his arms at his chest and stared daggers at Mr. Carysfort.

"Well, we can't let this incident pass as if it never happened, if that's what you were hoping to hear. Lady Sarah's been wronged by you, and there's only one recourse. You must do the right."

Perching on the very edge of her chair, Sarah glanced from Mr. Carysfort to the earl and then back to Mr. Carysfort. This was unfolding like a macabre nightmare in which she and the earl were nothing more than paper mannequins to be moved about at will by a greater force. Aunt Ophelia had never presumed to orchestrate her life, and having never answered to a father or a husband, she found Mr. Carysfort's attitude particularly galling. She was sure the earl must be equally as infuriated by their treatment. It was incumbent upon her to set matters right. "But Mr. Carysfort, you must not blame the earl." A terrible blush colored her cheeks. "He entered my room by accident, and I should have ordered him to leave, but failed to do so."

"And I suppose you, an innocent young lady, are also to blame for the improper activities that ensued."

Sarah ignored Mr. Carysfort's caustic suggestion. "Please, sir, let's not talk of blame. The important thing is I don't feel dishonored, nor do I wish to see anyone brought to task or forced to do the right. You know, it's not as if the half of England knows of this and the other half shall be reading about it in the morning *Times*. I shall never speak of the incident, and I'm certain the earl shan't either."

Radnor smiled. That was his sensible Lady Sarah, and knowing that she remained his ally he went to stand beside her chair. Perhaps if they presented a united front they would prevail. But his smile and his confidence faded when Lady Mornington next spoke.

"I'm afraid that's not exactly the case, Lady Sarah. Things aren't as tidy as they seem. While I told no one other than your aunt what I saw, it appears I wasn't the only one to see what transpired. Lady Anglesea, and my son, Reverend Wellesley, were behind me in the corridor and had the benefit of an unobstructed view once I'd crossed the threshold."

The earl cast a disbelieving glance toward the

ceiling and drawled, "Why do I get the impression I'm being bamboozled by my own family? In point of fact, dear Uncle Maximillian, this whole situation puts me in mind of more than one previous narrow encounter with the parson's mousetrap. Well, despite your attempt, Max, I won't do it!"

Lady Ophelia gasped. "How could you insult my niece with such a bald refusal?" She felt a monumental headache coming on. Oh, this was horrid, perfectly horrid. She didn't like any of this by half. From the start, she'd been uncomfortable with the notion of subterfuge, and now it appeared her reluctance was more than justified. The plan had backfired. Persons other than Lady Mornington had seen the earl in Sarah's room, and it was no longer a matter of knowledge between the two families. Furthermore, she and Lady Mornington had planned for the manageable scandal of the earl's unchaperoned presence, not for a passionate embrace reminiscent of the goings-on in a bagnio. It was of little account that said embrace made their argument for an immediate wedding all the more compelling. What mattered was that Sarah's reputation was truly in jeopardy, and while Lady Ophelia wished to see her niece married, she feared that if this plan were to fail, Sarah might forever remain unwed.

"Don't my feelings in this count?" asked Sarah.

"And how do you feel, my dear?" Lady Mornington humored Sarah.

"I'm not in the least insulted by Lord Radnor's refusal. He knows my opinion on marriage as well as you do, Aunt Ophelia, and you, too, Lady Mornington. Neither of us wishes to marry anyone or at anytime."

"Hah! And neither of you has the good sense the Lord gave you," was Mr. Carysfort's impatient retort. He stared at the pair of them, the pale-faced young woman perched on the edge of the over-stuffed cushion and the taut-jawed gentleman standing by her side, and he knew more than ever they were a perfect match, if in nothing other than stubbornness and defiance of character. Such perfection could not go unconsummated. Assuming his most unequivocal voice, he pronounced, "If you care one jot for Lady Sarah, you'll marry her, Beverly, and without hesitation or excuses."

"Of course, I care about Lady Sarah. She's intelligent, honest, and most sensible, and I have the deepest respect for her. But marriage is something else altogether, and it's because I respect her that I would not wish to shackle her."

His statement elicited a rapid succession of verbal abuse.

"Never heard such poppycock!"

"How can you say you respect her? Such reasoning is quite illogical, and I'd wager makes you a prime candidate for Bedlam."

"What about Sarah's reputation? That should be your primary concern."

At the mention of reputation the earl recalled that afternoon when he had raised the issue of the absent chaperone. Sarah had said something to the effect that most ladies feared for their reputations because gossip might harm their chances for marriage. He recalled her exact words, *But as I harbor no aspiration in that quarter, I have nothing to fear*. He also remembered what she had said about living without a man's guidance or intervention, and he was prompted to say, "Sarah, I believe, is best qualified to speak for herself on that matter."

"Have you lost your mind, Beverly?" demanded his grandmother. "I can't believe what I'm hearing. It's not for Lady Sarah to speak for herself. It's your place as a gentleman to take charge and set the proper lead in such a disastrous situation." She gave her head several dismal shakes. "How your father would blush at your conduct. It's shameful, and while I can hold no threat such as disinheritance over your head, I can pledge that should you fail to do the right thing and marry Lady Sarah, you will no longer be welcomed at Temple Radnor as long as I live."

Distress at such a rejection from his beloved grandmother laced the earl's plea. "Grandmother, please, you must—"

"Please, nothing. You are proving a gross disappointment, Beverly. No Carysfort has ever shirked his duty, however disagreeable that duty might be."

Sarah watched the earl wince. The dowager countess's remarks had hit their mark. Lord Radnor was a proud and honorable gentleman, and Sarah doubted he would be willing to support her at the expense of his family name. She also knew how much he loved and respected his grandmother and owing to those sentiments, he would place the dowager countess's sensibilities above hers in this matter.

"I'm very sorry about all of this," she whispered. Her voice was so soft the earl had to lean down to hear what she said. "I appear to have failed you miserably, my lord."

He gave her shoulder a reassuring pat, and Sarah,

who never cried, was, of a sudden, on the verge of tears. Her lower lip gave a hideous tremble, and she stilled it between her teeth as a horrible realization came to her. She wasn't upset for the earl's predicament, but for hers. It wasn't Radnor who was facing a fate worse than death, but it was herself. Sometime during the past weeks, the unmentionable had happened. Sarah didn't know why it required a calamity to confront the obvious, but with a new clarity of mind she realized the awful truth. Zeus and Minerva! She had fallen in love with the earl.

Precisely when it had occurred, she didn't know, but now as she stared into his Aegean blue eyes Sarah knew that love (and not their charade) accounted for her pique at the opera, and it was that same love which explained the quickness of her pulse whenever he was near. Perhaps it had been a reality from the moment he had landed at her feet in the Clock Court. Analysis in hindsight, however, was a futile endeavor; *it* had happened, and there could be no extinguishing the power of the tender emotion which had taken seed within her heart.

While Sarah had never planned to wed, she had likewise never planned to fall in love. Being of a pragmatic nature, she did not essay to deny the truth, and although the prospect of marriage to the man she loved should have filled her heart with joy, it didn't. Quite to the contrary, Sarah was aware of what the earl expected out of his marriage. An heir, and a wife, who neither cared nor complained when he went his own way. Before meeting the earl, Sarah could have imagined being a satisfactory wife, if those were the requirements. Now the prospect of being partner to such a barren arrangement didn't seem possible without untold misery. The expectation of virtual abandonment by her husband was perhaps the most ghastly future Sarah could envision for herself, and when she heard the earl capitulate to Mr. Carysfort's demands that they marry within the fortnight she feared her heart might break.

An urgent missive was hand delivered to Mr. Carysfort's second cousin, a clerical representative of the archbishop in Canterbury. A special license was obtained, the reading of the banns was waived, and six days later, on June 18, 1815, Lady Sarah Clement-Brooke and Beverly Edward Christian Carysfort, the Earl of Radnor, were married in a private ceremony in the Chapel Royal, Hampton Court Palace.

15

"**I** WILL NOT pass my wedding night in my uncle's guest room, nor in your aunt's apartment," the earl had informed Sarah the day before the ceremony. Hence, they departed Hampton Court in his lordship's drag less than twenty minutes after a reception al fresco had gotten underway in the Privy Garden.

It had been a perfect day for a wedding. Although a drenching storm had passed southward during the previous night, the morning had dawned clear and bright, and Sarah's spirits had risen to the occasion at hand.

Granted this wedding was not transpiring under the most favorable of circumstances, and granted, furthermore, she had never planned to marry, but this was her wedding day, and Sarah, ever pragmatic, was determined that it would be a time of happy memories. That resolve had been rewarded when a large bouquet of vernal roses had arrived with the earl's gold-edged card nestled among the velvety pink and white blossoms, and when he had held her hand throughout the ceremony, Sarah dared to harbor the hope these were signs their marriage would not be the emotionally barren arrangement she anticipated.

That glimmer of hope, however, began to fade when they climbed into the earl's sporty coach, and the hired driver wheeled the vehicle through the Lion Gates and down the mile-long avenue through Bushy Park. With the mauve brick palace behind them, the earl propped his back against the corner of the coach, stretched out his legs, and without a word to Sarah or so much as a glance in her direction, he proceeded to polish off a magnum of champagne.

The empty bottle lay on the velvet squabs. An uncomfortable silence stretched between the newlyweds. Any nodcock could fathom something was bedeviling the earl, and Sarah, suspecting she was the primary source of his ill humor, chose not to break the silence. The coach rumbled through the main street of Twickenham and on through Brentford.

Night fell. The interior of the vehicle darkened, and Sarah strained to detect any change in the earl's disposition. Studying his profile, she ascertained his eyes were closed, and for a moment, she thought he'd fallen asleep, but the steady tap-tap of one boot on the wooden floorboards belied that impression.

At length, he stirred, raising one hand to rake the hair off his forehead. He tilted his head in Sarah's direction, and she knew he was staring at her.

Sarah held her breath.

He spoke: "I know I'm a disappointment to you. Know you never wanted to be shackled with a husband, and I let you down." His words rang heavy with regret. For several days he'd been planning exactly what he intended to say to Sarah, but the script wasn't proceeding as planned. Again, he raked a hand through his hair in a gesture that revealed his anxiety and frustration. He'd intended this coach ride as the perfect time to be alone with his new wife and present his rehearsed speech, but, to Radnor's consternation, his nerve had floundered, and he'd found he needed the champagne to fortify himself. Now his alcohol-muddled brain couldn't recall his carefully chosen words. What Sarah deserved was his apology and his pledge to be the best husband he might given the circumstances. What she didn't deserve was some sodden confession, and he cringed at the sound of his thick voice.

"I let down my grandmother, y'know. Let down m'family name. Promise I won't let you down as a husband. You'll have your independence, dear lady wife. Fear not."

Something twisted inside Sarah's chest. Their marriage was to be precisely the sort of civil and impersonal arrangement she had feared, and while it was likely he expected her thanks for promising to respect her independence, she wasn't in the least bit appreciative. His pledge made her feel miserable and unwanted. No longer did she want the independence she'd once coveted with such vigilance.

She wanted the intimacy she'd observed between Aunt Ophelia and Mr. Carysfort; she wanted the closeness she'd begun to enjoy with the earl to continue, and mayhap to grow so that one day her husband might return a portion of the affection she held for him. Sarah was at a loss as to how to explain her feelings; she wasn't even sure she should do so. That closeness with the earl had been part of a growing friendship, not a forced marriage, and Sarah suspected their friendship was doomed to the fate of the mastodon. Why, she wondered with an increasingly heavy heart, did marriage have to change everything?

"And I, sir, shall do my part and endeavor not to disappoint you in any way," was her guarded reply. In point of fact, Sarah wished to do much more. She wished to please him, to make him proud to call her wife, and above all, it was her fondest wish to make him fall in love with her. Ever since that moment when she had recognized the true depth of her emotions for the earl she had been pondering what a marriage built on love would be like. There would be affection, companionship, trust and honesty, and knowing what happened whenever he touched her, she knew there would be passionate love-making.

One thought had led to another, and Sarah had begun to anticipate the night when the earl would make her his wife in every sense. It was no secret to Sarah that physical intimacy led to children, and while the thought of his warm searching lips, muscular arms and hard chest thrilled her, it was the prospect of a family that was most enthralling. Children and a family would bring them closer together and quite possibly lead to love. For that reason above all else, Sarah longed for this carriage ride to end as quickly as possible. The familiar trembling began in her limbs, but this time she was neither perplexed nor frightened. She understood and welcomed it.

Anticipating the night ahead and the possibility of winning her husband's love, Sarah shuddered with emotion. Through the darkness, she whispered, "You wish an heir, I recollect."

Radnor heard the tremor in her voice, he imagined a frightful blush upon her cheeks, and guilt stabbed at his conscience. She was being brave and noble, and he gave a silent curse that he had compelled this fine lady to endure such an intolerable set of circumstances. Oh, how she must loathe the thought of his touch, particularly since it was his lust that had brought them to this infamous point. He gave an inebriated nod. "Fear not on that account either. I will not force you to the marriage bed, dear lady wife. Not for awhile. Sooner or later I'll need an heir, but for now you must not worry."

There was absolutely no hope for the future. An odd hollow sensation burned in the pit of Sarah's stomach, and a single tear welled up at the corner of one eye to spill over and burn a hot path down her cheek. She turned away from the earl to stare out the window.

Moonlight bathed Sarah's face revealing the extent of her misery. Stark anguish marked her delicate features, and the earl watched as a tear trailed down her pale cheek. Desire and protectiveness, lust and tenderness washed through his heart and mind. He wished to pull her into his arms and wipe that tear away. Sweet Jesus, she was a beautiful bride in her mother's wedding dress of ivory chintz. How fragile she was in that old-fashioned gown. What a beguiling and tempting sight she presented with that high-waisted bodice accentuating her alluring figure. He desired to kiss her, to caress her, and yes, to make tender love to her. He yearned to comfort and please her. He needed to make her his wife in every sense of the word.

That not being possible he wished to ask, *Can't we at least remain friends?*, but he dreaded her reply. Despite what she'd said about not blaming him for what had happened that evening in her bed-chamber, despite her good nature throughout the whole of this ordeal, the reality was he had ruined her life, and he couldn't bear the rejection she was bound to deliver, the rejection which he rightly deserved. That she had sought to assume some of the blame herself only made matters worse.

The moonlight illuminated another teardrop as it coursed down her cheek, and he winced.

"I never cry, my lord." She essayed a denial in a small wobbly voice as she swiped that traitorous tear off her cheek with the back of her hand. "You must pardon me."

Acting on instinct, he extended a hand as if to take hers within a comforting grasp, but he stopped himself and let his hand fall to his side. Instead, he said, "It's been a long and trying day."

His wife deserved much more than he had to offer. Much more than any transitory comfort or mere apology. Verily, he had much to make up to Sarah, and right then and there the earl decided the best way to accomplish this would be to maintain his distance from her. Only then could he guarantee he wouldn't be driven to seduce, mayhap by force, his own wife. Only that way could he guarantee he wouldn't do anything to threaten her independence. He could see how miserable she was, and he didn't wish to exacerbate that unhappiness.

That night they slept in separate rooms in the master suite of the town house on Park Lane. In the paneled bedchamber that had been his father's and before that his grandfather's, the earl tossed and turned, his sleep tortured by images of Sarah in a state of undress, propped against a nest of pillows, her hair loose and flowing about her creamy shoulders, her eyes smoldering with desire and her lips parted for his.

Through a connecting door in a pretty room with flocked wallpaper, Sarah lay upon an embroidered counterpane curled in a protective little ball, her cheek pressed against the cool satin. She stared at the closed door that led to her husband's room. She had never felt as small and insignificant nor as uncertain of the future as she did in that strange room, and a renewed glimmer of hope was her only solace. Hoping that the earl had experienced a change of heart and would momentarily walk through that door, her ears strained to catch the slightest sound of movement from the adjacent room.

Time passed. Outside on the street the watch called four hours past midnight, but she heard nothing. The earl did not change his mind, and in the hour before dawn as she finally drifted into sleep, Sarah knew that this had been the loneliest night of her life.

On her first morning as a married lady, Sarah awoke to discover her husband had been up at dawn and had departed the town house shortly thereafter. Informed by his valet, Trebilcock, that he'd gone to George Street to meet with the Four-in-Hand Club, Sarah devoted her morning to exploration of the residence of which marriage had made her mistress. This activity required several hours as there were seven bedchambers with dressing rooms, a nursery, dining and breakfast rooms, plus the Adam's Room, the Winter Saloon, a formal receiving room on the second floor with a southern exposure, and the Downstairs Saloon, which had doors to the rear garden and whose windows were shaded by an ancient oak.

Below stairs in the kitchen, Trebilcock lined up the staff of fourteen, and after the necessary introductions, Sarah conferred with Mrs. Potts, the ancient, but thoroughly competent housekeeper. She assured the elderly woman she owned no intention of upsetting the established routine, and she complimented her upon the numerous artful flower arrangements that graced the establishment.

In the Adam's Room, Sarah browsed through the library collection that to her delight included Rousseau's *La Nouvelle Heloise*, translations of Grimaldi's essays on light transmission and the phenomenon of diffusion, and the complete Gibbon's *Decline and Fall of the Roman Empire*, including a valuable first edition of Volume I. These literary treasures, she was satisfied to note, had been regularly aired to protect them from mildew, a tribute to Mrs. Potts' housekeeping skills.

From the Adam's Room, she went to the walled garden at the rear of the house. There she admired the fish pond with statuary and the arbor of jasmine fragrant roses sheltering a wrought-iron bench. It would be a perfect spot to relax with one of those books. It would also be a perfect spot, a rather bold and unfamiliar inner voice declared, for a romantic rendezvous, and Sarah found herself blushing at the suggestive direction of her thoughts.

In the afternoon, she napped, and upon waking, she instructed the cook to prepare a sizable tea for herself and Radnor beneath the rose arbor. If the garden inspired thought of romance, she might as well test that theory. But the earl didn't return home until after dark, having engaged in a curricle race to Salt Hill, and the jellied sandwiches hardened, the platter of fresh scones went untouched, and an endless queue of ants trekked through the bowl of sugar crystals.

The next day began in a similar vein. Again, she rose to learn her husband had departed; this time, for his club in St. James's. But this time, following a hearty breakfast of shirred eggs and porridge, Sarah mustered her morale by reminding herself that as a mature and independent adult there was no reason why she must idle about her husband's town house. As she herself had pointed out to the earl, she did not require a gentleman's guidance or approval to live a full life.

Having made up her mind to make the best of the situation, she penned a brief missive to Miss Wellesley, who had departed Lady Mornington's apartment at Hampton Court and was residing at Apsley House, the residence of her great-uncle Lord Wellesley at Hyde Park Corner. She invited the younger lady to join her for an afternoon outing in one of her husband's numerous carriages. The earl's footman waited for Miss Wellesley's reply, which was in the affirmative, and at half past four o'clock, Sarah instructed the coachman to take her round to Apsley House.

"How glad I am to see you, Lady Sarah, I mean Lady Radnor," Miss Wellesley corrected herself as she settled into the seat beside Sarah. They were riding in the earl's landau, and the weather being agreeable, the hood had been folded back.

"Oh, please, you mustn't bother with such protocol. Won't you simply call me Sarah?"

"I should like that, but only if you call me Eugenia."

"Of course, I shall." A parade of vehicles drove past Apsley House and into Hyde Park. It was nearing five o'clock. "Well, Eugenia, the whole world seems to be bound for the Park. Shall we join them?"

"How can you ask? Don't we wish to be *fashionable*?" quipped Miss Wellesley.

"That depends." Sarah matched her companion's light-hearted tone. "I've heard fashion involves something rather *rotten*."

Miss Wellesley laughed. "Then we must join them, if we wish to determine what constitutes fashion and how rotten rotten may actually be."

The coachman wheeled into the line of vehicles, and the ladies found themselves amidst a spectacle of beautifully appointed carriages with footmen attired in lavish livery, their occupants dressed to the nines in the latest styles, including, of course, several outfits from Madame Tizou. Among the carriage company were the *crème de la crème* of the polite world, plus a few females Sarah suspected ranked among the *demi-mondaine*. Too, there were a few young ladies and numerous gentlemen on horseback. Among them Sarah recognized Sir Benjamin and the Earl of Conyngham, and she acknowledged their greetings with a demure nod. At one point, the earl's coachman paused to allow them to chat with the passengers of a *vis-à-vis*.

"I'm pleased you invited me on this outing, Sarah," Miss Wellesley declared when they resumed the circuit. "And although I shall sound most dreadfully selfish I must confess to being vastly relieved for the escape. My uncle's household is intolerably glum with all the talk of war with Bonaparte."

Sarah offered an understanding smile. "I don't think you selfish. The prospect of war is abhorrent, and endless discussion of war must be most discouraging. It's quite natural to wish to take one's mind off the danger our army faces. In fact, I suspect your great-uncle Arthur would not wish his family to go into premature mourning. Didn't he himself plan to attend the Countess of Richmond's ball?"

"Of course, you're right, but—" Miss Wellesley's smile faltered, and she whispered, "The talk is worse than ever. Couriers from the Foreign Office arrive on the hour. As we speak there may even be a battle. And then . . . then mourning shall, indeed, be the order of the day, and you know how that is. Plans get canceled and . . ." she broke off, unable to speak the words aloud.

"You're concerned that your wedding shall be postponed?"

Miss Wellesley nodded. "I know it's shameful of me."

"Hush. You must not berate yourself." A little

frown lined Sarah's forehead. Would Aunt Ophelia's wedding be delayed? That would be most unfortunate. On the other hand, had her aunt been devoting her attentions to her own marriage plans instead of focusing upon Sarah's affairs, she might already be wed. Mayhap Aunt Ophelia deserved such a postponement, came Sarah's wholly uncharitable thought. Before she might check herself, she said, "In fact, as far as I can discern this marriage business isn't all it's cracked up to be." This hasty remark elicited a flicker of dismay upon Miss Wellesley's countenance. Sarah hastened to add, "Oh, Eugenia, *you* musn't worry about anything. That was a horrid thing for me to say, and I'm sorry. I'm certain Viscount Strabane shall be a model husband and your marriage shall take place as planned, and it shall be everything you've always dreamed."

"But not yours? Not the earl? I don't understand, Sarah. Your wedding seemed quite the most romantic of events." Miss Wellesley had numbered among the small group of guests at the ceremony, and the sight of the tall and darkly handsome groom holding his bride's hand had caused her to cry like a watering pot. In addition, the couple's hasty departure from the reception had left their friends and relations with the distinct impression that they were eager for privacy. Miss Wellesley sighed. "Rather dreamy, in fact. I know the viscount loves me, but I can't imagine *him* transgressing the norm to wed by special license. How I long for a ceremony as private as yours without a gaggle of persons one hardly knows to stare and wish one well as if they cared. And all those flowers on the refreshment table. Oh, Sarah, it was beyond beautiful. It was magnificent. I've never seen so many roses. There must have been twenty or thirty dozen at least." She gave another sigh.

"Things are not always what they appear," said Sarah as she commenced to explain the actual reason for the nuptials. She concluded on a somewhat sardonic note, "At least we appear to have succeeded in our purpose. If no one suspects we were motivated by something other than true love, my reputation remains intact. Aunt Ophelia and Mr. Carysfort can be pleased with their accomplishment in that regard."

"But this is dreadful. So very sad." Miss Wellesley was personally stricken by Sarah's disclosure. "Don't you care about the earl at all?"

Sarah cast a quick glance about the park as if to ascertain whether any of the passing equestrians could overhear their conversation. Her voice dropped to a stage whisper. "I care very much and wish above all else the situation were different. Have you any friendly advice, Eugenia? I've scant experience in matters of the heart."

Pursing her lips in speculation, Miss Wellesley considered her new friend's predicament. "Having no more experience than yourself, I can't speak from personal knowledge, but I do know an irrefutable source of advice. At times like this, I ask myself what Lady Mornington would advise."

"Pray, what would your great-grandmother recommend?"

"I'm sure she'd say that if you wish matters to change, then you must be the one to take the initiative." Miss Wellesley lapsed into thought once more, then expanded, "Nothing momentous, mind you. Keep it simple. When the opportunity arises, you might ask the earl to take you for a drive. That sort of thing. Anything which might put the both of you together more often so that in time he'll come to consider your marriage in a different light."

"You're right. Such an approach does sound like Lady Mornington. It also sounds like something my Aunt Ophelia would recommend, and it might succeed, if he was ever around."

Miss Wellesley cogitated another moment, then she grinned. "I can just hear what my great-grandmother would say to that. Give the earl a gift then he must seek you out to extend his thanks. And that will be your first opportunity to let him know you wouldn't spurn more of his company."

Sarah was willing to try almost anything, and the next afternoon, she visited Berry Brothers in St. James's to obtain a gift for the earl. The shop was famous for its choice teas and coffees, and knowing her husband's fondness for the stronger blends, she decided to select something special for him. It would not be an extravagant gift, but one that evidenced consideration.

The shop smelled of tea and coffee, curry, paprika and mustard seed. Along the back wall, there was tobacco from the New World, and in lidded glass jars there were spices from the Far East, the colorful and pungent powders creating a mysterious atmosphere. Dark wood shelves were lined with canisters of Congue, Pekoe, Souchang and Bohea, and there was an assortment of ornate tea chests on the countertop. There was a chest painted with peacocks and several with a scroll and ivy pattern, but she passed those by, choosing instead one which depicted a gentleman atop a high-perched phaeton, racing down a country lane, a pack of cavalier King Charles spaniels in pursuit. It was a delightful scene, and Sarah was certain the earl would like it above all else. As the proprietor filled the chest with rolled green gunpowder leaves, a heavy-set gentleman, his cheeks florid from exertion, rushed into the shop.

"Good afternoon, Lord Grey." Mr. Berry looked up to address one of his oldest and best customers. "You've left the City early today, and in rather a hurry, I see."

"Incredible news, Berry. Incredible news. Mr. Rothschild's courier has brought word."

Sarah and the other customers focused their attention upon Lord Grey.

"News?"

"On the stock exchange?"

"No, not on the exchange. It's Bonaparte," clarified Lord Grey. "The Frenchie devil's been defeated."

"You're sure of this, sir?" Mr. Berry's anxious tone was mirrored upon the faces of his customers. Since sunrise there had been rumors of a battle somewhere in Belgium. A great battle the likes of which no man or woman could comprehend. No one in London, high born or low, had not heard the tales. The French were routed. Tens of thousands lay dead and dying. Trebilcock had brought Sarah the story at noon; he'd heard it from the earl's stable boy, who'd heard it from a lad who worked for a gentleman in the Foreign Office.

"Well, it may not be in the papers nor posted at Mansion House yet, but I'd stake by Mr. Rothschild any day," said Lord Grey. "I was at the coffee house on Threadneedle Street, and they said Wellington's defeated Bonaparte, and Mr. Rothschild's making a killing on the stock exchange."

"Bonaparte defeated? When?" this from an elderly gentleman.

"Where?" inquired a lady standing by the spices.

"Someplace near Quatre Bois. Waterloo, I think it was, and about two days ago, they're saying."

"And the victory, was it hard won?"

"I couldn't say, ma'am, but official word should be coming any time."

"I must hurry home," the lady by the spices pronounced. "My daughter's husband is in the Second Life Guards. She shall be paralyzed with worry."

"Indeed, ma'am, you should go to your daughter, and I shall close the shop early," declared Mr. Berry. "At a time such as this, one should be with family." He handed Sarah the wrapped package, and she hurried outside to the waiting landau, but the vehicle was nowhere to be seen.

Sarah had left instructions with the coachman to wait for her, but in the brief time she'd been inside Berry Brothers the atmosphere on the street had gone through a dramatic alteration. No longer were carriages lined up at the curb, their drivers snoozing beneath caps, pairs of matched cattle gnawing their bits. No longer did ladies attended by their footmen stroll down the avenue while dandies strutted their stuff, and an occasional flower-er girl called out to a passerby. Of a sudden, the whole of London had flooded out-of-doors, the street was an undulating sea of pedestrians eager for confirmation of the rumored victory, and Sarah was swept up in that tumultuous wave of humanity as it pressed toward Whitehall.

16

CLUTCHING HER LILAC silk parasol and the wrapped tea chest, Sarah tried to move in the direction of Park Lane, but found it quite impossible to make the slightest progress. The crush of bodies surrounding her presented a force as immovable as a fortress wall, and she didn't possess the strength to surmount it.

Someone's elbow knocked Sarah's bonnet askew, and before she might right it, the hat fell off to dangle by its satin ribbons down her back. Another elbow jostled her and she lurched forward to find herself sandwiched between two heavyset boys, whose familiarity with soap and water was evidently nil as they reeked of grime and sweat and day old ale. She gagged, raised a gloved hand to cover her nose, and in doing so, dropped her parasol. The last she saw of the ruffled silk creation it was quickly turning brown beneath the onslaught of trampling feet. The noise and chaos were frightening in the extreme; it seemed as if she were trapped in a maelstrom from which there was no exit, and Sarah experienced an unfamiliar shiver of fear.

Up ahead a horse nickered causing a momentary improvement in her spirits. Perhaps the earl's landau was returning for her, and she stood on tiptoe to discern in which direction to head. Her next emotion, however, was not relief. It was aggravated apprehension when she saw a farmer attempting to direct a team of work horses through the throng.

Somewhere in that mass of humanity, a woman screamed, "Get 'old of yer 'orses!"

The crowd surged away from the on-coming vehicle. A very heavy someone stepped on Sarah's toes, and a small cry of pain escaped her lips.

"Sarah!"

It was the earl's voice. Strong and clear, and oh so glorious to hear. Again, she rose up on her toes to scan the sea of heads.

"Over this way, Sarah. Over here."

She espied him on the other side of the street and waved at him. The crowd pressed closer, and in the next instant, she lost sight of all except the top of his beaver hat, but his voice reached her.

"Try not to move. I'll get to you," he called out as he forged through the rabble.

The earl had not seen his wife since their return to Town, and while it was not his usual style to devote time to the contemplation of any female, Sarah had not been far from his thoughts since their wedding night. He had missed her these past two days. Now he struggled to make his way to her, and when he reached her side, he pulled her into his arms as if it were something he'd done a thousand times before.

"Thank God, you're safe." The earl stared down at Sarah, his blue eyes caressing her face. The color had drained from her complexion, her bonnet was dangling by its ribbon, and her hair was in disarray, yet she had never looked lovelier. Gently, he brushed the stray curls into place.

Sarah's heart somersaulted. Her violet eyes sparkled. A touch of pink returned to her cheeks, and she said the first thing that popped into her head, "Good afternoon, my lord."

The simplicity of her greeting was wholly unexpected amidst the turmoil, and the earl responded with a robust laugh. "It is a good afternoon, isn't it? But what in heaven's name are you doing out now?" Drawing her into the safety of a nearby doorway, he placed his tall form between his wife and the crowd to shelter her from the frenzy.

"I was shopping." Sarah felt the tea chest pressed between them, and she was seized by the most incongruous sense of anticipation. She couldn't wait to give him the gift, couldn't wait to see the expression upon his face when he unwrapped the tea chest and saw the beautifully painted carriage and finely drawn team of cattle. She repeated herself, "I was shopping. I never dreamed to be caught up in all of this."

"Where's Henderson?" he referred to the coachman of the absent landau.

"Lost I supposed." She couldn't resist flashing a bantering smile.

Radnor could not remember a time when a smile

had seemed so immeasurably sweet, and there in that cramped doorway, surrounded by a hundred strangers, the earl's entire outlook toward his marriage altered. He had been maintaining his distance from his wife, in part for fear of her censure, and in part to shield her from himself, but staying away from Sarah was not what he wanted. It was what he'd thought was right, and now he was forced to question whether he had made the right decision. Now for the first time, he could dare to believe there was a chance their marriage might be something other than two independent-minded persons going their separate ways.

"Come along with me, Sarah," he said her name easily. "There's a tavern with a private parlor around the next corner. We can wait there 'til the crowds disperse."

Just then the Tower guns roared over the Thames, and in St. James's Park the jubilant salute of gratulation was echoed by the ceremonial guns from the Horse Guard Parade. Church bells pealed, and to the south, orange and red rockets criss-crossed the night sky over Vauxhall.

"It's official. Victory at last!"

From Kensington to Limehouse huzzas spread through the alleys and avenues of the metropolis. Lord Bathurst had received a dispatch from Wellington that chronicled the events of 15 June through the decisive battle on 18 June. Bonaparte and his army were, indeed, defeated, Wellington had taken one hundred and fifty pieces of cannon, and the victorious allied forces under their commanding general and the Prussian Blucher were marching toward Paris.

A few paces from Sarah and the earl a group of young bucks broke into song. *Rule Britannia*, they chorused, and the crowd joined in on the refrain. Men and women alike shed tears, and there was more kissing than beneath the mistletoe at Christmastide.

The earl leaned down to whisper in her ear, "Years from now when our grandchildren ask where we were at this moment in time, we shall have quite a tale to tell them."

Speech eluded Sarah. The elation of the moment was exhilarating, but her husband's mention of grandchildren cloaked her in a palpable euphoria. Sarah gazed up at the earl, and electricity charged the air as they wordlessly stared at each other. It was an electricity she could feel and almost touch, an electricity she could see as surely as the rockets blazing above the rooftops. She had never felt as close to anyone as she did to him at that moment, and she knew that this memory, not that of her wedding day, was the remembrance she would always carry in her heart.

"I shall treasure the recollection of this moment forever," she murmured as instinct took over and she snuggled up against her husband.

The earl took the brown paper package from Sarah, then wrapped an arm about her shoulder to lead her through the crowd to The Two Black Cats. The innkeeper showed them to the private parlor, and the earl ordered bowls of leek soup, warm brown bread with cheese and a bottle of sherry.

"And how are you finding Town life?" he asked once they were settled.

Feeling at ease, her reply was forthright. "I can't say it's entirely to my liking, but I have enjoyed an outing with Miss Wellesley. She's proving a friend and I hope to see much more of her as time passes."

He nodded. "I'm glad to know you've been busy."

Recalling Miss Wellesley's advice, Sarah seized upon this opportunity. "Miss Wellesley and I went on a carriage ride in Hyde Park," she began, then paused to take a sip of sherry to fortify herself. "Perhaps you might wish to join me next time."

"Your invitation is appreciated." He smiled, scarcely daring to believe the good will he detected in her voice. "But I believe I've an even better idea. How about a real ride? Not some sedate wheel through the Park at the fashionable hour, but a jaunt in my high-perched phaeton to Salt Hill."

"You'd take me?" She couldn't keep the surprise and disbelief from her query. A tiny smile turned up at the corners of her mouth, and pale rose tinted her cheeks at the prospect of sitting beside her husband and clutching his arm as they raced along a country road.

"Of course, I'd take you. Why ever not?" He liked the rather shy way Sarah grinned at his invitation, and he enjoyed the way the rising color upon her cheeks revealed her pleasure. Wishing to observe an increase in that happiness, he added, "I could even teach you to handle the ribbons, if you like, that is."

Her responding expression was more than he could have hoped it might be. It was beyond radiant; it was celestial. "Oh, I'd like that very much, indeed."

"Good." He poured more sherry into her glass.

"What are your plans tomorrow?"

"If that's an invitation, nothing I can't cancel."

"Excellent. We'll leave after breakfast."

For well over three hours, they sat by the window watching the goings-on outside. The earl ordered a second bottle of sherry, and they talked about his grandmother, who had returned to Temple Radnor to ready the estate for their arrival at the Season's end, and they compared notes on the latest plans for Lady Ophelia's and Mr. Carysfort's wedding. When at last the crowd in the streets began to thin, they departed on foot for Park Lane.

It was nearing ten o'clock when they reached the town house, and despite the brisk walk through the cool evening air, Sarah was suffering the effects of too much sherry. Her footing was unsure and she leaned upon her husband as they ascended the front stairs to the vestibule.

"Thank you," she whispered, clinging to his arm.

"What ever for?"

"For everything. For rescuing me in the midst of the pandemonium, and for the pleasant and wholly different evening." She swayed to one side and a tiny giggle escaped her lips. And thank you, she thought with a giddy rush of joy, for the promise of our future. Thank you for returning to me the dream of the possibility of your love. She took a steadying breath and tilted her head to meet her husband's gaze. "I look forward to our drive, my lord."

He stared down at her, his blue eyes were bright and warm, and his gaze so intent it seemed as if he were committing her every feature to memory.

Somewhere in the depths of the town house a clock chimed the hour, and when silence once more fell about them, he spoke, soft and low, "Sarah, won't you please call me by my name? We must not be so formal, you know. Let me hear you say it. Say my name."

A tiny skirl of pleasure raced up Sarah's spine. His words touched her as surely as a caress, like velvet they tempted and seduced her senses, and high crimson brushed her cheeks at this overture toward intimacy. "I look forward to our ride, Beverly," she said with a shy smile and a hopeful leap of her heart. How simple it was going to be after all to set her marriage on its proper course. Miss Wellesley had been correct; she had merely needed to be with her husband for their relationship to turn in a better direction. The past few days could be forgotten; tomorrow was going to be the first day of her married life. Again, her smile burned radiant as she gazed up at her husband. A peculiar husky quality laced her voice. "Thank you, Beverly."

Something tightened deep inside the earl. Sweet heaven, how he longed for her. How he ached to claim her for his wife, but she was under the influence of that blasted sherry, and he knew it would be wrong to take her to their marriage bed this night. His name so sweetly uttered was all the treasure he could receive this night. Resigned, he led her upstairs, sat her down on the end of her bed, and rang a maid to assist her. Then he went to his room, and wishing that he hadn't let her imbibe to such excess, he locked the connecting door that separated them.

*   *   *

In the morning, Sarah rose early. It was like a miracle. That hollow spot inside her was gone. She rang her maid, had the package from Berry Brothers taken down to the earl's place at the dining-room table, and foregoing her usual cup of chocolate, she hurried through her toilette so she might join her husband for breakfast before their outing to Salt Hill.

Ten minutes later she entered the dining room, but it was empty. That morning's copy of *The Times* with Wellington's dispatch to Lord Bathurst printed in four full columns across the front page had not been touched, and beside the newspaper lay the unopened gift from Berry Brothers. She took her seat and sipped her Belgian chocolate, glancing every now and then to the door, waiting for her husband's entrance.

Trebilcock entered instead. "Pardon me, my lady, I've a message for you from his lordship."

"Yes, Trebilcock," she asked in a bright tone, expecting to receive a note, but there was none.

"Lord Radnor asked that I convey his regrets. He was called away on a business matter and shan't return until late afternoon."

"Thank you, Trebilcock," she said in a curiously steady voice. *A business matter*, she thought bitterly, biting her lower lip and thinking how lamentable it was that she had deceived herself. How foolish she had been. Last night, for the space of several wild hours she had started to believe that her husband might be able to return her love, but, in truth, last night had not changed anything. Radnor's life was still separate from hers. There were people and places and things that consumed his time and attention about which she had no knowledge, things which he did not choose to share with her.

Unable to eat anything more than a nibble of dry toast, she slipped outside for a solitary walk. How strange the empty streets seemed after last night's revelry. Gone were the jubilant hordes, and the only sound was the hollow clip-clop of hooves on the cobbles. Following Curzon Street to Piccadilly, Sarah wandered in the direction of the Mall. Up ahead, a crowd milled outside Mansion House where a placard had been posted. Sarah moved near enough to read the proclamation:

Mansion House, Thursday, June 22, 1815
Notice having been given that the Public Offices will be illuminated Friday and Saturday evening next, in consequence of the late glorious Victory.
The Lord Mayor recommends to the inhabitants of this City to defer illuminating their houses till that time.

Sarah frowned. She wasn't in the mood to celebrate. What she wished was to turn back time and pretend that the events of the past twenty-four hours had not occurred. She would go home and be the wife that Society and her husband expected her to be. She wouldn't complain about his unexplained absence, nor would she reveal her disappointment that he had let her down. She would be quiet and meek and behave in such a way that presented no impediment to his pursuing a separate life. Such behavior on her part was, she owned, cowardly and quite contrary to every independent-minded, self-respecting bone in her body, but it was painless. To pretend all was well meant to cease hoping for change, and only then might she be able to get on with her life.

"Good morning, Lady Radnor," a somewhat familiar voice interrupted Sarah's reverie.

She turned to see Lady Diana Ryder and her cousin the Marquess of Egremont. She forced a polite smile. "Good morning, Lady Diana. Lord Egremont."

The marquess peered to Sarah's left, then to her right. "You're not out and about on your own, are you, Lady Radnor?" he queried with feigned concern.

"Of course, she isn't," Lady Diana declared, casting a quelling look upon her cousin.

Egremont ignored Lady Diana. "I could have sworn I saw Radnor riding in the other direction less than an hour ago," he mused aloud.

Sarah felt as if the ground had opened beneath her. Her heart plummeted, and that horrible empty spot burned worse than ever in the pit of her stomach as she fought to maintain an untroubled expression. The thought that anyone might be privy to the less than perfect circumstances of her marriage was lowering in the extreme; that someone as petty and vicious as Lord Egremont might know more about her husband's whereabouts than she pierced her heart with excruciating pain. Enduring a loveless marriage promised to be difficult enough, but to be subjected to this sort of gossip would make the loneliness intolerable. She mustered her wits and parried, "You must be mistaken, sir. My husband

and I planned an outing this morning."

Lord Egremont shrugged as if to say, *Claim what you like, I know what I saw.*

Lady Diana was mortified, and she addressed Sarah with genuine sincerity. "Allow me to offer my felicitations, Lady Radnor. While the announcement of your marriage was certainly a surprise, it is nonetheless one of several reasons for celebration."

"Oh, don't be a nodcock, Diana," drawled Egremont. There was a taunting edge to his affected voice. "It wasn't a surprise at all. Was it, Lady Sarah?"

Sarah opened her mouth to repudiate the marquess. She intended to denounce his rudeness, but knowing her anger would only be more gossip for this petty tattlemonger, she held her tongue. Indeed, if she were a gentleman she would have called him out for such an open insult. That not being possible, she spoke in her most buttery voice, "My husband and I have always agreed that surprise is the essence of life." She schooled an innocent smile. "Being as certain as you are of the future, Lord Egremont, your life must be intolerably dull. You have my deepest sympathies, sir."

Lady Diana giggled, then sobered when the marquess took a firm grip of her arm to lead her away. Winking over her shoulder, she called back to Sarah, "I hope I shall have the pleasure of seeing you again, Lady Radnor. Do come to call upon me while you're in Town."

"Thank you, Lady Diana. I shall," Sarah replied, and as the pair disappeared around the corner, her anger and hurt and resentment bubbled to the surface.

No, she wouldn't go home and behave as if everything was all right. She wouldn't act as if this sham of a marriage was what she wanted, nor would she act as if her husband's behavior was acceptable. Because it wasn't, and there was no reason why she should have to pretend otherwise. She refused to be the object of speculation or pity. She refused to endure a life of lies and posturing for the benefit of some unspoken set of socially acceptable rules.

Never before had Sarah conformed to Society's expectations, nor had she been one to cower at a little bit of untoward gossip, and it would be dishonest to start acting like someone else. She had been wrong to suppose that marriage changed everything. It didn't. Not really. She was still the same unconventional Sarah she had always been, and first and foremost, she had to remain true to that self.

She would not go home and demand an apology and an explanation from her husband. It would be pointless, for his actions made it clear that he did not wish to be accountable to Sarah. He had promised to take her to Salt Hill, but had instead gone about his own affairs. His actions made it clear that he expected his wife to live her own life, and as Sarah had been doing that for years, she decided to pick up where she'd left off. Before her erstwhile husband returned to the town house that evening, Sarah intended to be on the road and half-way to Hampton Court, and at least, she would sleep that night knowing that she had been true to herself.

17

THE CAPRICIOUS ENGLISH summer descended upon the metropolis, and the Season, owing to the sad reality that hardly a family among the upper ten thousand had not suffered a loss upon the field at Waterloo, drew to an unusually abrupt close. At Hampton Court, Sarah endeavored to ease her aching heart by concentrating upon her latest pursuit of palace ghosts. Lady Ophelia travelled to Temple Radnor to visit the dowager countess while the earl and Mr. Carysfort remained in Town. At Strabane Hall, Suffolk, Miss Wellesley, thanks to the intervention of the Countess of Mornington, was allowed to wed the viscount in an unpublicized ceremony. (While her parents had opposed the ceremony, her great-grandmother had made the brilliant proposal that the young couple devote the first months of their marriage to founding a bettering society for children who had become fatherless as a result of the battle.) And on 15 July, Bonaparte surrendered to Captain Maitland of the *H.M.S. Bellerophon*.

But it was not this much-awaited intelligence which captured Lord Radnor's ear as he dined with Mr. Carysfort at Boodle's on the evening of the fifteenth. It was his wife's name trumpeted by that doddering fool the Earl of Beauchamp to his ancient bosom bow de Montfort which caused a fork of roast pheasant to halt before his parted lips.

"*Lady Radnor* and *Captain Stallings*?" Beauchamp spoke in the sort of monotone over-loud voice that was peculiar to the hard of hearing. At a near-by table, Lord Radnor winced when the elderly gentleman coughed into his fist as if to attract an audience before he repeated, "Lady Radnor and Captain Stallings? Never heard of the gentleman."

De Montfort's tenor was no better. While neither gentleman harbored the intention of addressing the full membership of Boodle's neither could hear worth a farthing, and to make matters worse, de Montfort's eyesight was so poor he viewed the world as if looking through the wrong end of a telescope, a phenomenon which created the impression that his dinner companion was seated several yards distance from him. He yelled across the table, "Yes, his name's Stallings. Lady Radnor and someone by the name of Stallings. Believe there are some Stallings in Derby. Youngest son took up with the Life Guards or some such regiment. Mayhap that's the chap."

"So the gel's been seeing a good deal of him, you say."

"Indeed, and I must admit I'm surprised." Their

conversation volleyed back and forth like thunder to echo about the dining room. So boisterous was their exchange that no one in Boodle's that night could be accused of eavesdropping, and even the waiters, usually stone-faced, blushed at this shocking lack of discretion while Lord Radnor himself was present. De Montfort blasted on, "Though Radnor always had a way with the petticoat line, can't say I expected him to marry and allow his wife to carry on in such ramshackle fashion. Thought he'd keep a wife under better rein. Y'know, if I didn't know better I'd say he was following in Conyngham's footsteps, and I never did have a jot of respect for *that* fellow."

At this insulting remark, Radnor allowed his fork to fall beside his uneaten breast of pheasant with a clatter. His jaw tightened, and disgusted and robbed of his appetite, he pushed the plate away.

Mr. Carysfort, who had been observing the play of emotions cross his younger relative's face, was both alarmed and concerned at the uncharacteristic vulnerability which the earl's expression revealed. He addressed de Montfort's tasteless remarks as gently and tactfully as was possible. "The old goat's got a point, y'know. It is a bit out of character. Can't say I ever expected *you* to be the sort of complacent husband who'd put up with—"

"Being a cuckold?" the earl cut him off, his voice heavy with self-mockery.

"Well, I wasn't going to put it quite *that way*. You're being rather too harsh on yourself, Bev. Besides which you don't know if any of it's true. God knows they might actually be talking about Lady Redding or Lady Ander, both sound vaguely like Radnor, and there's no telling with those two relics."

The earl's reply to this attempt to minimize what they had heard was an unintelligible series of grunts.

Mr. Carysfort went on, "What I was going to say before you interrupted was that I never expected you to be so, well, so resigned to such a dismal state of affairs. You in Town; Sarah at Hampton Court; and rumors flying about the both of you. By virtue of doing nothing, you're as much to blame as Sarah when it comes to causing tattle. Why, it's positively apathetic of you. Most peculiar. And regardless of the reason for your wedding, you're acting like nothing matters. Not the family name or your marriage or how either of you might feel in any of this. Fact is, the Bev I knew would have taken himself off to Hampton Court long before now and put a stop to the whole of it."

"And you're right on the mark, Max. I would have ridden hell for leather across the heath and delivered an ultimatum to that sorry woman who might call me husband. But, you see, that fellow never expected to care a whit for his wife, he never expected that sorry woman to be Sarah, and he would have found delivering ultimatums quite painless."

"Aaah," was Mr. Carysfort's response to the earl's enlightening statement.

"Precisely. I find myself in a devil of a pucker. You see, while that particular fellow never thought to care for his wife, I find I care for Sarah. I don't like seeing her hurt, and having already made a royal botch of her affairs, I don't wish to make any more bungles, if I can avoid it. Oh, yes, I've wanted to go out to Hampton Court, and in the worst way. A day hasn't passed that I haven't wished to see Sarah, to hear her laugh and share a lazy afternoon stroll with her like we once did. By God, if only I could go out there to know for myself what's happening and try to set things right between us. But, no, I can't. Given my existing record, I'm sure a visit to the palace would develop into nothing more than another gross blunder on my part."

This discouraging conclusion required some serious consideration from Mr. Carysfort. He and Lady Ophelia had wished their younger relatives to be wed for more than one reason. Personal motivations aside, they had sincerely believed the pair was well-suited, and it grieved them to watch as the wedding upon which they had placed all their hopes seemed to be leading to nothing but loneliness and despair. In fact, that was one of the reasons for Lady Ophelia's visit to Temple Radnor; she hoped the dowager countess might suggest a remedy to the ugly impasse that was developing between Sarah and Beverly. Mr. Carysfort picked up his wine glass, twirled it by the stem, finished the remaining Bordeaux in a single sip, then said:

"You know, Bev, I think you're going about this all wrong . . . thinking it's best to keep your distance. You'd do better to consider it in a wholly different light. Think of it this way. What's worse? Doing nothing—as you are now—which seems to set the course of your marriage on a downward spiral from which there might never be any improvement or recovery. Which, if you care about Sarah, is hardly what you wish to occur. Your alternative must be to take some action." He set the wine glass on the table and leaned toward the earl to empha- size his final words. "The truth is you haven't the foggiest notion what Sarah wants, and don't say it's clear from her actions or what she may have said two months ago 'cause it ain't clear at all."

"She did pick up and leave Town." Having experi- enced a profound and unfamiliar sense of rejection upon learning Sarah had quit the Park Lane town house, his ego did not wish another rebuff.

"Which proves nothing. You know very well one can't evaluate the present based on the past. Cir- cumstances change. People change. Besides which I seem to recall your making a credible case for Sarah being the one best qualified to speak for Sarah. Something to the effect that you've no right to go about deciding what it is she wants or thinks."

Once more Beauchamp's monotone resounded through the dining room. "Well, y'know those Clement-Brooke women. Educated and outspoken." He gave a dramatic shudder.

Again, the waiters flushed carmine. Mr. Carysfort gripped the arms of his chair, the earl's face dark- ened, and de Montfort answered with an affirmative nod. "A mighty queer lot."

"Indeed, the lady might at least behave with a bit more discretion. Why, they've hardly been married a full month, and already she's gallivanting about like a free spirit."

"Free and shameless."

"What's that?"

"I said *shameless*. Lady Radnor's quite shameless. Don't you agree?"

There no longer being any doubt as to whom the

elderly gentlemen were discussing, Radnor tossed his serviette on the table and rose from his chair.

Max put out a hand to stop him. "Bev, no. You mustn't."

"Egad, did you think I'd challenge that wizened old vulture?"

"There is a rather ominous look in your eyes. Homicidal, in fact."

The earl managed a snort of laughter. "You can put your worries aside, Max. I wouldn't waste my energy on Beauchamp or de Montfort. No, I'm bound for the palace. My good wife, I believe, has much to answer."

The first of the black Hamburgh grapes were ripe, and the earl found Sarah in the palace structure that housed the celebrated Great Vine. At the head gardener's urging she was filling a basket with the succulent deep purple berries, and upon entering the glasshouse, the earl's pent-up anger was immediately diffused by the sight of her. He paused inside the doorway and neither announced himself nor moved toward Sarah, choosing instead to appreciate her loveliness from afar.

Sweet Lord, she was more exquisite, more desirable than he recalled, and there was a responding ache deep inside him. He drank in the pretty picture of her slender form garbed in an unadorned cambric gown. There was nothing artificial or lofty about his wife; she was feminine and alluring and quite, he mused with an unexpected flight of frivolity, adorable. He watched in delight as executing a half-turn, she stood on tiptoe to reach one of the higher lengths of vine and her bonnet fell back offering a partial glimpse of her face. The earl grinned. Her lips were redder than usual, almost the same dark purple color of the grapes, and her delicate fingers were also stained with the juice. How like Sarah to have forgotten to wear gloves, how like her to be caught like a schoolgirl with traces of grape juice upon her lips, her chip bonnet dangling down her back like an errant curl. This was the Sarah he had come to see; the Sarah he had missed.

For Sarah, it required monumental discipline not to spin all the way around to face the earl, but instead to continue plucking grapes as if she were the only one present. From the moment Radnor had entered the glasshouse a sixth sense had enveloped her. She was certain he was there, and this intuitive suspicion was confirmed when she raised up on tiptoe to see his reflection in the glass. Her heart skipped a beat. Although the tall image was no more than a shadow, there was no doubting it was her husband. She could tell by the broad square shoulders, the above-average height, and when he tilted his head to one side she recognized that aristocratic profile. Hermes. He was here at last, and her heart swelled with anticipation. What message might he have for her?

In as natural a fashion as possible, she turned the rest of the way round. "My lord, good afternoon. What brings you to the palace?" Sarah asked, trying to appear nonchalant, allowing no more than the hint of a smile to tease her mouth and eyes.

He doffed his beaver hat and walked toward her. "To see my wife," was his initial reply with the responding flicker of a smile. He reached her side and drew in his breath. Yes, she was lovely, and she was his to hold and to cherish, not some errant captain's. His smile faded. On a sobering note, he added, "And to find out if the stories are true."

"I'm sure I don't know what you're talking about," Sarah countered with feigned ignorance. Leaving Town had been difficult and waiting at the palace had been even harder. It hardly seemed possible that he was here. "Stories?"

"Captain Stallings." The name dropped from his lips as if it were a fatal poison.

"Ah, the good captain," she said slowly, almost secretively. "A most brave and noble gentleman. He was gravely wounded in battle. Perhaps you have heard."

More venom crept into his words. "And you've been offering him all the comforts he might need to recover."

"I suppose you could say that." In truth, the good Captain Stallings had been deceased for more than one hundred and fifty years. An officer in Cromwell's army, he had been buried alive beneath the pavement stones in the Fountain Court. It was his spirit, Sarah assumed, which haunted that wing of the palace, and she had devoted the past weeks to sighting the captain. Her ultimate goal was not merely to confirm the legend of the entombed Roundhead officer, but to hopefully assist him in ceasing his decades of howling and wandering. "Do you object? After all, the gentleman is quite desperate for comfort."

At her casual, almost challenging tone, the earl's left eye brow arched. He drawled, "I had heard stories."

"About the captain?"

"About *you* and the captain."

"I see." She lowered her lashes to prevent him from detecting the sudden spark of expectation in her eyes. Was that jealousy in his voice? The past weeks had been interminable, causing Sarah to doubt whether her absence had in any way affected her husband. She had even wondered if the carefully dropped tidbits regarding herself and the captain might have fallen on deaf ears. She went on, her voice moderated with measured caution, "It was not my intention to offend you in any way, my lord, but I was under the impression we had a civil arrangement between us. You know, you go your way and I go mine. I saw so little of you in Town that I thought it best to return to the palace to pursue my own interests."

"Ah, yes, well, I know what, what," he floundered for a second, "what it was I once said to you. But, you see—," the sentence broke off in uncertainty.

"Yes, my lord?" Sarah encouraged.

"Well, you see, I'm no longer sure what it is I really want of a marriage. I mean I used to know, or at least I thought I did, but things have changed." Egad, what was wrong with him? He was babbling like a fool ready for the wards at Bedlam. Of course, things had changed. He was married and not of his own choice. Married to a woman he loved but who—

Love?

Caught off guard by this silent admission, his mind momentarily went blank. Christ's nails, that was it! He had fallen in love with Sarah, and his fear of returning to the palace had very little to do with male ego, it had everything to do with the unexpectedly fragile condition of his heart. He loved his wife, and even more than wishing her happy, he found he owned the wish that she might love him, too. Momentarily robbed of the ability to speak, he stared at Sarah acutely aware of her beauty and of the sudden sensation in his chest that was this alien thing called love.

Sarah spoke in gentle reminder, "I recall that you did say you wished an heir at some time," and he imagined he could detect a note of encouragement in her voice.

Still unable to utter a single syllable, and overwhelmed by the realization of his love for Sarah, he continued to stand before her, his hat in one hand, the collar of his shirt suddenly excruciatingly scratchy. Somewhere inside the glasshouse a bird flapped its wings, the leafy fruit-laden vine overhead rustled, several grapes plopped to the ground, and time stretched between them. A cold sweat broke out over his body, he pulled at the shirt collar and required a deep breath before he might ask:

"Are you suggesting that now is the time to start a family?"

She blushed. "Is that your wish, my lord?"

Of course, it is! he wished to shout at the top of his lungs. *Of course*! But he knew he must prove himself deserving, and now was not the time for such declarations. His voice dropped another octave, his words were husky with emotion. "I did think we might spend more time together. Before all this— the wedding, I mean—I had come to imagine we were friends of a sort, and well, it seems a shame that that should stop. I did enjoy our afternoons together here, y'know, and I should like to spend time at the palace again. With you." There, he had said it. Well, not all of it, but it was the best he could do. He had made the commitment to renew their friendship, and in time, he would hopefully be able to offer and in return ask for more in their relationship.

She plucked another bunch of grapes, offered him one and then popped a single round fruit into her mouth. He watched in fascination as her lips closed over it, and he waited none too patiently for her to finish and respond to what he had said about wishing to spend time with her.

Her grape-stained lips arched upward into the most enchanting smile he had ever seen. "I think that's a wonderful idea, Beverly. I'd be most pleased to have your companionship again."

The earl exhaled a pent-up breath. His facial features relaxed, and his heart thudded a hard tattoo against his chest. By God, yes, he loved this woman. He loved her smile and the sparkle in her violet eyes, he loved her humor and intelligence, and he loved the way she blushed. Curious and dauntless and unselfish, she was a lady without parallel, and he loved her for all those reasons and more. There was much he wished to say and do, a world of revelations and tender whisperings to share with her, but he thought it best to go slowly, to court his wife and prove himself worthy of the love for which he yearned. In a voice that fell as soft as a caress, he dared to say, "If it's agreed I'm home to stay, then perhaps my wife should properly welcome me."

This was the encouragement Sarah needed, and
without hesitation, she raised on tiptoe to kiss her
husband. It was a short sweet kiss delivered not
quite upon his lips, but upon his jawline just below
the corner of his mouth. The rough texture of his
skin was intoxicating; it alluded to the full potential
of his masculine strength, and Sarah sighed. He
reveled in her sweet response and the lingering
scent of spring roses, and they both cherished the
secret fantasy that this moment marked the true
beginning of their marriage.

The next two weeks were idyllic ones spent discussing scientific and philosophical articles of mutual
interest and working together on a presentation for
the local historical society on the evolution of the
palace orchards. They enjoyed several excursions
through the nearby countryside upon which occasions Sarah learned to handle the ribbons of the
earl's curricle, while from Sarah, the earl learned
the art of creating wax tracings from the intricate
mantlepieces in the oldest Tudor apartments of the
palace. At last, Sarah gave her husband the tea chest
she had so lovingly selected, and the earl was more
than properly appreciative. He thanked her with a
pearl choker and a sporty curricle of her own.

There was no mention of Captain Stallings or
the unfortunate circumstances of their wedding,
nor did they discuss what the future might entail.
This halcyon interlude was marred only by the
lurking presence of Lady Charlotte Harrowby, and
two contrived fainting incidents in the Chapel Royal. One scene in which Miss Camilla Burges Watson
again landed in the earl's lap requiring that he carry
her outside, and another in which some theretofore

unknown miss from the West Country managed the same feat of timing and placement the very next Sunday.

Each evening after dinner, it became their habit to stroll through the scented grove of lime trees on the east front of the palace. On one particular night when they reached the river, rather than retracing their steps, they proceeded along the promenade erected by William III. The walkway, some six hundred yards in length, ran parallel to the Thames and was marked at intervals of fifty yards by magnificent seven-foot-high wrought-iron gates. A full moon in a heaven replete with a thousand silver stars illuminated their way.

"How impressive these gates are," the earl remarked when they passed beneath one whose chief ornamentation was the initials of William and Mary entwined with thistles.

"I've always thought so." Sarah paused to gaze up at the gate. "I'll tell you something I've never told another living soul. Not even Aunt Ophelia. These gates had a special role in my childhood."

"Yes?" He hardly dared to believe how she was opening up to him, hardly dared to utter that single gentle word of encouragement.

"When I first came to the palace I spent hours by the river. This was a perfect place for a lonely child with its tow-barges and teams, the noisy flocks of geese and swans, and the little boys on the opposite bank fishing for barbel, but more than all that it was these gates I loved. I used to imagine I could climb up to the heavens and be with my mother and father again. Just being here made me feel closer to them, and not quite so sad or lonely."

He allowed a few moments to pass. "This is the first time you've ever talked of your parents."

" 'Tis not for want of love, for I hold their memories close to my heart," she said continuing to gaze past the top of the gates and toward the heavens. "Father always impressed upon me the importance of dwelling in the present, not in the past. He would wish me to continue to cherish my memories and use them as a foundation for my future. Although it's been many years, I still think of them often. When I was young it was the quiet moments before bed that I recalled; the times when my mother would sing to me or my father would hold me on his lap and tell me stories about ancient civilizations. Then, as I grew older those memories changed. Now I find that what I most especially recall is the love they shared."

"Tell me about it," he urged.

"Oh, it was very romantic," she began in a wistful voice. "They were always holding hands and whispering, sharing secrets that made Father laugh and Mama blush. But, you know, I never felt left out, rather their contentment and joy made me secure. They were best companions, too. I can see them sitting side by side on the marble bench in our garden in Peshawar, planning a new adventure together, and never dreaming to leave the other behind. On the rare occasions when my mother didn't accompany my father, I recall how impatiently she waited, pretending not to be distracted from our game of draughts, dressed in her prettiest gown and smelling of lemon soap. And I remember how she would cry and exclaim upon his arrival, and how he would share every detail of his travels with her. I think he loved the way she sat on the edge of the chair to listen, and I know he loved her more than life itself. As a child it seemed an unbearable injustice to lose both one's parents at the same time, but it was rather a miracle, for neither would have survived without the other. I think that from the moment they first met their souls must have been united for eternity."

For a few minutes the earl could not speak. Sarah was still staring heavenward, and he watched as she blinked and star-bright teardrops spiked the edges of her eyelashes. Softly, he asked, "Is that the sort of marriage you wish for?"

"Yes, Beverly, it is." She used his name easily now, but the pleasure he derived each time it flowed softly from her lips had not diminished. "Although for the longest time I merely thought it was something lovely meant only for them, not ever for me. Now I feel otherwise, or at least I *hope* otherwise." She turned away from the night sky, and her eyes met his. Slowly, meaningfully, she reaffirmed, "Yes, that's the kind of marriage I would like for myself."

Her words hung upon the air between them, expectant, inviting, electrifying, and oh, so seductive, and when he moved toward her she responded as if drawn by a magnet into the waiting cradle of his arms. He drew her closer and pressed her firmly against his hard chest, then holding his breath, for fear of having gone too fast, he waited to see what she might do.

Sarah's heart pounded furiously. She had longed for this, dreamed of the moment when he would again hold her as he had done in her bedchamber, when he would again kiss her as a lover does his mistress. This was what Sarah wanted from her husband, and there was no hesitancy in the way she tilted her face upward to meet his descending mouth. There was nothing but the promise of unfolding passion in the way she trembled at the sensations his warm firm lips aroused. His kisses covered her eyelids, her cheeks, and moved from the sensitive hidden spot behind her ear to the base of her throat where her blood pulsed.

One of his hands found its way to the bodice of her gown, and he began to caress her. A small moan escaped her parted lips. There was something oddly unsatisfying about the way her breasts began to ache, and she moaned at the exquisite agony of not being able to get enough of these pleasurable sensations.

"Shall we return to the apartment, Sarah?" he whispered low, his question causing her to tremble anew.

She nodded in agreement, he replied with a deep chuckle, and as they walked toward the great mauve palace the earl knew this was the night Sarah would finally become his wife.

18

SARAH'S BED WAS empty. The satin counterpane and eyelet sheets had been turned back, her nightrail set out by the maid, but neither the linens nor the white lawn gown had been touched by their mistress.

"Christ's nails!" the low curse escaped the earl's mouth that had gone taut with anger. When they had returned to Lady Ophelia's apartment he hadn't followed Sarah directly to her chamber. He had allowed her the privacy he assumed a lady desired before he would join her, and although he hadn't stated his intention to make love to her that very night, he was certain she understood what he'd meant when he suggested they return to the palace. To add a special touch to the evening ahead, he'd taken a few extra moments to go to Max's apartment for a bottle of sherry. He never expected to enter Sarah's

216

chamber—the bottle raised in invitation, a seductive smile upon his features—to discover Sarah wasn't there. It was a rude and wholly unpleasant shock.

He yanked the tapestry bellpull on the wall, and when the maid didn't come running, he walked to the door and yelled into the corridor for the hapless young girl from Teddington whom Sarah had hired as a maid of all trades.

Groggy-eyed, the village girl appeared, a shawl hastily drawn about her shoulders. She bobbed the semblance of a curtsy. "Yes, milord?"

"Where's your mistress?"

"Why, milord, 'tis Captain Stallings. I thought for certain you knew that. Thursdays is always the captain's night."

"What?" He gave his head two violent shakes as if to make sense of this unsettling information. "Where are they?"

"The Fountain Court, of course."

"Of course," came his cynical retort. "How could I have forgotten?" Reason eluded him, and as he stalked out of the apartment a single thought became his mind's focus. Sarah was *his* wife, not the concubine of some wounded war hero, and as his wife she should pass the night with him, not offering comfort to another man. The earl loved his wife, he wanted her, and as far as he was concerned he had waited long enough to claim what was rightfully his.

"Beverly, what ever are you doing behind that post?" Sarah detected a movement behind one of the statuary pedestals and required only a second to recognize the tall broad-shouldered figure of her husband. "I never expected to see you here. This is a surprise."

Upon returning from their walk, she'd been disappointed when he hadn't come to her bedchamber, and having assumed she'd read too much into their embrace by the river, she decided to go ahead with her regular Thursday night vigil. It was far better to be occupied with something to divert her mind, rather than to lie in bed, wishing and hoping for the impossible as she had done on her wedding night.

The earl stepped out from behind the marble column, and Sarah smiled, but her smile faded when he spoke.

"I've come to take you back to the apartment."

"What?" His abrupt tone startled her, indeed, it was most disconcerting. Even if she had read too much into their kiss, they had parted on a warm note, and she could imagine no explanation for his drastically altered mood. "Have I done something to displease you, Beverly?"

He winced at the familiar use of his name. Did she call the captain by his christian name too? "I'll not tolerate another day of this."

"*This*?" Sarah was truly confused.

"Yes, this." He gestured about the court. "My wife and Captain Stallings. I've had quite enough of the talk and insinuation. Where is he?"

There was something about his tone that infuriated Sarah. Yes, she was hurt that apparently he didn't trust her, and she was crushed that the closeness she had sensed growing between them was gone. But more than either of those emotions she was angry that he could take such an arrogant tone with her. It was the same tone he'd used the night they had met in the Clock Court, and she didn't like it one iota. He made everything sound as if he was perfect while she, on the other hand, was irredeemably flawed.

"*You'll* not stand it? And what of me?" A vision of the past two weeks idyll marred by the fainting incidents in the chapel and the lurking presence of Lady Charlotte crossed her mind's eye. "Ladies continue to throw themselves upon your path with abandon. Am I supposed to pretend that I enjoy my husband being the object of every female's romantic fantasy?"

"And why not? Everyone knows our marriage is naught but a mockery."

"You blame me?" Her voice began to quiver.

His jaw tightened. How could she sound so damn innocent? "Your conduct, madam, certainly lends full credence to the assumption that I'm—let us say—somewhat available for dalliance."

She slapped him. It happened quickly before she might stop herself, and in the next instant, she gasped in horror as red fingerlike streaks appeared upon his cheek. Their eyes met, and she gasped anew at the raw fury etched upon his hardened features.

"That, madam, was a grave mistake." His left hand whipped out to grab her wrist and pull her to him, and his right hand clamped the back of her head as his mouth claimed hers in a hard vengeful kiss.

Sarah's eyes watered. Whether they were tears of pain or humiliation she neither knew nor cared as she struggled to free herself from his hold. "No, not like this," she cried, trying to wedge her arms between her chest and his to push him away. "No!" She shook her head from side to side as if to deny the brutality of his touch. Finally, she succeeded in breaking free, and she stepped back, raising a trembling hand to her swollen lips, her chest rising and falling from exertion. "How could you?"

The pain and confusion upon Sarah's face was an unbearable sight. It tore at the earl's conscience, and registering the full impact of his impetuous action upon his wife, he cried out, "My God, what have I done? Forgive me, Sarah. I have no right. None at all. Forgive me."

"Of course, you have the right," she declared. His words, hinting at a reserved indifferent relationship, horrified her more than his rough touch ever could.

"Perhaps," he conceded on a weary sigh. "But it doesn't give me leave to behave like a rutting beast. Fear not, Sarah, I shall never do such a thing again, and while you've no reason to trust me, you must believe I speak the truth. I'll never touch you again."

This solemn vow of abeyance was the last thing Sarah wanted from her husband. She wanted closeness and love, tenderness and a family. Earlier this evening, such a reality had seemed within reach, now it was slipping from her grasp. The prospect of continuing with a loveless marriage was more than she could bear, and for the first time in her life, Sarah surrendered to a fullfledged bout of shoulder-wracking tears.

Profoundly shaken by the sight of Sarah's breakdown, the earl threaded both hands through his hair. Egad, this was the muddle he'd sought to avoid. He was hurting dear Sarah even more than he already had. Of a sudden, the past two idyllic weeks evaporated, and the only reality was the pain he was inflicting upon his sweet wife. He reached out to her, but withdrew his hand in uncertainty.

"Please, Sarah." Her muffled sobs pierced his heart as clean and searing hot as a statement of loathing would have done. "I don't wish to hurt you."

"Then why do you distance yourself from me?" she managed to ask between teary gulps of air. "Why since our wedding night have you erected a space between us?" This last question was wrenched from her, the words laden with despair and confusion, and the earl was so discomposed by this stark revelation of unhappiness that he required several moments before he could reply.

"Because I thought it was right," he said, knowing that although this was the truth it sounded stupid and holier-than-thou, and it certainly couldn't be what she wished to hear.

Sarah considered this explanation. At least he hadn't said something like, *Because that's what I wanted* or *I was too busy to find time for you*. Mayhap there was, after all, reason for hope, and throwing caution to the wind, no longer caring about who spoke first, and only wishing to be honest and have done with this charade, she rejoined.

"You *thought* it was right to treat me like a stranger? Your wife? To take the word of others over mine? Indeed, never once to ask me how I might feel or what it is I might want or need. At least not until this night when we talked about my parents, but that must have been a mistake. A sorry slip of the tongue." A bitter edge crept into her voice. "Was it a mistake, Beverly, to allow yourself to treat me as a living breathing woman? Is that it? It was a mistake, and now you're punishing me for your mistake?"

He stared at her. High color dotted her cheeks, her eyes flared with emotion. The depth of her passion and indignation was as astounding as it was unexpected, but no more so than what he thought it was she was trying to tell him. "But what about Captain Stallings?" he wondered aloud.

"I don't know," she shot back with a disgusted shrug. "Maybe he'll roam the palace for another hundred and fifty years. I seem to have failed in providing even a dead man with the slimmest degree of satisfaction."

A ghost. Stallings was a ghost. Feeling as if the earth had just moved beneath his feet, the earl gaped at Sarah as the enormity of his error settled over him. What a fool he'd been. She was right to berate him. "I had no idea," was his quiet response.

Sarah blushed. Her voice too assumed a hushed quality. "I know you didn't, and I'm sorry, for the truth is it was I who dropped more than one misleading morsel of gossip about myself and the captain."

"But why?"

"In the hopes I might make you jealous."

"You wished me jealous?" He sounded as incredulous as a schoolboy who'd thought he was bound for a caning only to discover he'd been tapped for the most prestigious prize-day award.

"Of course," she said gently, and as the anger evaporated from her expression it was replaced by the ethereal sort of sweetness associated with new love. Her countenance radiated tender affection. "Don't most women madly in love with their husbands wish to be the center of their attention and that they might cause their husband to turn every shade of green imaginable?"

She had said it, and she held her breath waiting for his reaction. Indirect though it might have been, she had nevertheless talked of her love. This was it, the moment in which her entire future would be determined. She had everything to lose, and when he finally spoke she wasn't disappointed.

"I suppose they do, but no more so than husbands who are madly in love with their wives."

"Are we saying the same thing?" she dared to ask.

"I think so." He reached out to cup her chin in his hand, his thumb caressing the space below her lower lip. "I love you, Sarah. I adore you, I desire you, I need you."

This time, tears of joy welled within her eyes. "And I love you, Beverly." She stepped closer, and when he pulled her to his chest to cradle her against his shoulder and run a hand across her back in a gentle caress, she nestled against him feeling as if her heart might burst with happiness. She sighed and tilted her face upward in order to meet his eyes. "Might we turn back the clock an hour or so?"

"That's a splendid notion with which I wholly concur." He dropped a kiss upon her forehead, then slipped his arm about her waist. "Sarah, sweet lady wife, are you ready to retire? Are you ready to be mine?"

As if on cue, the moon slipped from behind a cloud to reveal an impish look of adoration mingled with flirtation upon Sarah's face. "I'm ready, my lord. Quite ready to be yours, Beverly," she added his name on a husky whisper that hinted at the lifetime of passion that would be theirs.

L'envoi

THE *H.M.S. BELLEROPHON* sailed to Plymouth harbor on the Devonshire coast where its imperial prisoner became an object of much curiosity. Men, women, and children flocked to the coastal town, and boarded hired boats which encircled the ship to wait and watch for Bonaparte to take his daily walk about the deck. Then on August 4, the *Bellerophon* departed Plymouth to transfer its prisoner to the *Northumberland*, a larger St. Helena-bound warship.

Two days later another private wedding ceremony was conducted in the Chapel Royal at Hampton Court Palace. Lady Ophelia Clement-Brooke was married to Mr. Maximillian Carysfort, and as the couple stood before Reverend Wellesley one of the guests in the front pew sniffled into a lace handkerchief. It was Sarah, who was finding herself unaccountably teary-eyed of late, and although she bit her lower lip to control herself, it was the strong arm of her husband wrapped about her waist that saved her from an unladylike public display of emotion.

She tilted her head upward to smile at Beverly. His hold about her waist tightened, and he returned her smile with that lazy grin which would always make her heart lurch.

"Do you think they'll be as happy as we are, sweet wife?" he asked in a whisper, his velvet-smooth voice hinting of the new-found passion that was a part of their particular happiness.

Sarah blushed, then nodded an affirmative reply. Reverend Wellesley declared Lady Ophelia and Mr. Carysfort man and wife, and the groom kissed his bride. On a meaningful note, Sarah added, "Faith, they shall be most ecstatic, and without the detours we were forced to endure."

The earl chuckled. "Tell me, sweet wife, will I ever be able to live down my infamous past?"

"You already have, Beverly, and in a most unique style," she said, her gaze moving to the rear of the chapel to rest upon a small brass plaque by the door. The morning after their reconciliation in the Fountain Court the earl had instructed the palace housekeeper to post the following unusual notice:

> "Whereas a tendency to faint is becoming a preva-lent infirmity among young ladies frequenting this Chapel, notice is hereby given that in the future ladies so afflicted will no longer be carried out by the Earl of Radnor, but by Branscombe the dustman."

Sarah recalled the surprise and joy she had experienced when he had shown her the notice. Albeit somewhat oblique, it was the final evidence of the strength of his love. Again, tears misted her eyes, her nose prickled, and observing the play of emotion upon his wife's face, the earl knew a responding tightening in his chest.

"I love you, sweet wife," he whispered, leaning close to her ear, the words falling warm and gentle as a caress upon her skin.

She shivered and turned until she faced him. Her wide violet eyes sparkled. "And I love you, Beverly."

Forgetting entirely where it was they were, Sarah allowed her husband to pull her into an embrace, and she met his descending mouth with sweetly parted lips.

At the chapel door, the newlywed couple paused to face their guests. "Happy, my love?" Mr. Carysfort whispered in his lady's ear.

"Of course." She looked at her husband, then at her niece, who was locked in a passionate embrace with the earl, and for the first time in many years, she experienced the sensation of owning not a care in the world. "Blissfully happy, dear Max. It's all turned out just as you predicted. The summer's not yet over and already I've had my fondest wishes fulfilled."

"So there's nothing else you want?"

"Well, mayhap a grand niece or nephew would be nice."

Mr. Carysfort tossed back his head in full-bodied laughter. "From the look of things, my dear, you may not have to wait over long for that. Might I suggest by the end of next summer? Would that be soon enough?"

"Perfect." She gave his hand a squeeze and they proceeded into the chapel yard, where their guests joined them all except the tall ebony-haired earl and his petite wife. The younger couple had slipped out the side entrance and retired to their apartment for the remainder of the afternoon.

Avon Romances—
the best in exceptional authors and unforgettable novels!

THE EAGLE AND THE DOVE   Jane Feather
76168-8/$4.50 US/$5.50 Can

STORM DANCERS   Allison Hayes
76215-3/$4.50 US/$5.50 Can

LORD OF DESIRE   Nicole Jordan
76621-3/$4.50 US/$5.50 Can

PIRATE IN MY ARMS   Danelle Harmon
76675-2/$4.50 US/$5.50 Can

DEFIANT IMPOSTOR   Miriam Minger
76312-5/$4.50 US/$5.50 Can

MIDNIGHT RAIDER   Shelly Thacker
76293-5/$4.50 US/$5.50 Can

MOON DANCER   Judith E. French
76105-X/$4.50 US/$5.50 Can

PROMISE ME FOREVER   Cara Miles
76451-2/$4.50 US/$5.50 Can

Coming Soon

THE HAWK AND THE HEATHER   Robin Leigh
76319-2/$4.50 US/$5.50 Can

ANGEL OF FIRE   Tanya Anne Crosby
76773-2/$4.50 US/$5.50 Can